ROOMMATE RMPS

Crave Thy Neighbor

TEAGAN HUNTER

Editing by Editing by C. Marie

Proofreading by Judy's Proofreading & Julia Griffis

To me,
You did it.
Be proud of yourself.
Now go eat some pizza.

Chapter 1

MAYA

I am completely screwed.

Well, not *completely*, because I can't get *screwed* screwed to save my life.

Okay, fine. Not to save my *life*, just to save my vagina from developing cobwebs.

I'm getting way off track here...

I nibble on my thumbnail, a disgusting habit I really should give up, and stare at the email pulled up on my laptop screen.

TO: WEST_MAYA@MAILFLOW.COM
FROM: LEASINGLAUREN@WHITEOAKAPT.COM
SUBJECT: APPLICATION STATUS

Dear Ms. West,

We regret to inform you your application for the two-bedroom apartment at WHITE OAK APARTMENTS has been denied for:

NO AVAILABLE UNITS

We thank you for your interest in being part of the WHITE OAK APARTMENTS community. We wish you the best in your apartment search.

Lauren Stein
  Leasing Manager

It's not the first email like this I've received, and I'm sure it won't be the last.

In the last six weeks since I received notice from my landlord that the building is being sold and demolished, I've put applications in on anything I can find.

Unfortunately, since everyone else in my building is doing the same, and due to the fact that we live in a small Colorado town where the supply of affordable living is already scant, well…the pickings are slim.

It's been one big game of hurry up and wait, and I'm almost out of time to wait.

My lease will officially be terminated at the end of the month. If I can't find something soon, I don't know what the hell I'm going to do with myself and my almost-thirteen-year-old son when we're scraping by as it is.

I navigate back to my inbox and click on the email from my landlord.

TO: WEST_MAYA@MAILFLOW.COM
FROM: DAN@DANFORDAPARTMENTS.COM
SUBJECT: EXTENSION

Ms. West,

I wish I had a better reply for you, but my hands are tied. The deal has been finalized and there's no possible way to extend it. The buyer was clear: all occupants must vacate the premises by the end of the month.

Please know this decision was not made lightly. Trust me, if I could have told him to screw off, I would have. The last thing this town needs is another outdoor sports equipment shop.

I've not made this public knowledge, but being a single mom yourself, I'm sure you'll understand…Katlyn is sick, and unfortunately, the medical and medication bills are stacking up. Selling wasn't what I wanted, but it's the best solution I can come up with for my daughter.

You've been a great tenant over the years, and I'd be happy to write you a letter of recommendation should you need one.

I'm sorry about this. Please let me know if I can do anything.

Best,

Dan Ford
Danford Apartments Owner

Like it did the first, second, and third time I read his email, my heart sinks.

Hell, it breaks for him.

Katlyn and my son, Sam, are the same age. I can't imagine watching Sam going through anything that would cause him pain.

I'd sell the damn building too.

It's hard to be angry at him, which sucks because I could use someone or something to be angry at right now.

"Crap, crap, crap," I chant, bouncing my head off the back of the couch a few times.

I lay my head against the cushion, stretch my neck toward the sky, and blow out a long breath.

What am I going to do? I have nowhere to go. Either nobody has apartments available or, if they do, they are out of my price range or out of the school district. I've checked out a few houses, but most are on the outskirts of town and not in the best shape or are owned by people I do *not* want to be renting from. If all I had to worry about was myself, fine. I could manage it. But with Sam in tow, I can't take on a potential problem like that.

I wish I could afford to buy us a house, but I don't have money for a down payment.

My best friend, River, offered to let Sam and me move in with her and her boyfriend, Dean, until I could find a place, but three adults, a teenager, and two pets—one being a cat who is a major asshole—sharing a small, two-bedroom apartment? So not a good idea. We'd all kill each other within a day or two.

Since my parents are out of the question entirely, my only other choice is my ex-husband, Patrick.

If I needed to—like I had zero other options—I could go to him. He wasn't the best husband, but he'd never reject me if I needed help. Except the last thing I want to do is go running back to him and show him I've failed on my own. Just picturing the satisfied grin on his face has my stomach aching.

Tears sting my eyes, and I do everything I can to fight them off. The last thing I need is for Sam to walk in here and see me crying. I've worked hard to be strong for him throughout the years, and I'm not going to change that now.

That's right.

I'm *strong.*

Hell, I managed a teenage pregnancy all on my own when my parents wanted nothing to do with me. Finding a place to live with the deadline inching closer and closer? Piece of cake compared to that.

I lift my head, determination coursing through my body.

I can fix this. I'm not sure how, but I can.

"Yo, Mom, what time are you leaving?"

Speaking of my teenage pregnancy...

I snap the laptop closed before he can see what's on the screen. I don't need to bother Sam with this stuff. It's my problem, not his.

I push up off the couch and move toward the kitchen, shoving the computer back into my bag where it hangs off the chair at the bar. Sam knows getting into my work bag is prohibited, so I know it's at least safe from his prying eyes in there.

"Why? Curious how much longer you have on your GameStation?"

"Mom." He huffs, rolling his eyes. "It's a *Play*Station, not a GameStation."

"Roll your eyes at me again and I'll take your *Game*Station right back to the store."

He starts to lift his eyes skyward again, then thinks better of it when I raise my brow at him.

"Sorry," he mutters. "What time is Dad getting here?"

I glance at the clock on the stove. "He said he'd be here about six thirty."

"Cool. Can I get ice cream after dinner?"

"You'll have to ask your father."

"He'll say yes. He always does."

Of course Patrick always says yes to ice cream. He's the cool parent.

We share custody of Sam. Oftentimes he'll spend a week at my place and then a week at his father's.

And oftentimes he'll come home with shiny new gadgets or telling me about all the cool stuff he did with his dad.

I try not to be jealous of all the things Patrick can provide, but it's hard sometimes.

"Just make sure if you're going to play your game, you're doing it out here. I know how wrapped up in it you can get, and I don't need your father knocking on the door for several minutes disturbing the neighbors."

I've received that complaint before from the always-angry lady next door, and I don't care to get it again. I have other things to be worried about.

"I will."

"Good." I press my hands against my stomach. "Okay, how do I look?"

I opted for a simple yet trendy outfit for the night out: an off-the-shoulder, long-sleeved silky dark pink blouse plucked straight from a mannequin at the small boutique I work at, a pair of dark-wash skinny jeans, and black booties. It's nothing that will turn heads, but it's cute enough to get me through a couple of hours with my friends as we nurse a drink or two and complain about life.

"Beautiful."

I grin at him because he's not saying it to be a kiss-ass. He's just that sweet. "That's why you're my favorite kid."

"I'm your *only* kid." He sighs like he's exhausted by me.

"Thank god, too. I couldn't handle another one of you." I cross the room and wrap my arms around him, pressing a kiss to the top of his head. He grumbles, trying to wiggle out of my embrace. "Love you. Be good for your dad. Text me when he picks you up, please."

Patrick's supposed to do that too, but he always forgets.

Sam never does.

"Love you too," he mutters, and I tousle his hair as he tries to shove my hand away, but I don't miss the grin forming at the corners of his mouth.

He might almost be thirteen and is convinced he's a grown-up, but he's a momma's boy at heart. He always has been. We bonded during all the years I stayed at home with him.

I grab my purse off the hook by the door and slip it over my body, then give myself one more glance in the mirror.

I tousle my own hair and smooth down my shirt again.

Eh, good enough.

I'm not trying to impress anyone tonight. I just want to drink and have fun with River.

I need a break. Need to let loose.

I will not think about how I only have weeks to find a place to live.

Drinks. I need drinks.

I've known River White since we were eight years old. We've been best friends since the day she moved into the house next door and have been through every major life event together. We run a business together. See each other almost every day.

There is no doubt she knows me better than anyone else in this entire world.

So why she believes I want to go for drinks at a hole-in-the-wall, dingy *sports bar* is beyond me.

But here I am, pulling open the door to Hole in One and stepping into the crowded room. Almost all the tables are occupied, and I only spy a few empty spots at the bar.

I do a quick sweep, not seeing River anywhere, then head toward the bar, squeezing onto one of the few empty stools and flagging down the bartender. He nods, letting me know he'll be with me in a moment, and returns his attention to the couple in front of him.

I pull my phone out of my purse and shoot off a message to River.

Me: Are you sure you told me the right place? There's A LOT of sports crap on these walls…

River: Unfortunately, yes. Dean loves it for some godforsaken reason.

River: GIF of Judge Judy rolling her eyes

River: We're running a little late, just so you know...

River: SORRY

Me: You're totally having sex, aren't you?

River: Well, not right now, no.

River: But we might have...

Me: GIF of Rachel from *Friends* **saying** *I'm so happy and not at all jealous*

River: You know you love me.

Me: Right now? You're like my fourth favorite person.

River: Top 5, baby!

River: Be there soon. **kissy-face emoji**

I set my phone to vibrate and slide it back into my purse to resist any temptation to spend the whole evening on it being disappointed when I come up empty-handed.

The cab ride here was spent scrolling through apartments, and I only came up with one new listing in a place on the line of the school district. I bet if I made enough of a stink, I could keep Sam in his current school. I filled out the application and sent up a prayer.

It's about all I can do right now—keep hoping *something* lands in my lap. Positive energy and all that mumbo jumbo.

The only thing I'm positive about right now is needing a drink.

Where the hell is the bartender?

I spot him at the other end of the bar, talking with a different customer now. He looks like he's going to be a while. I let my eyes drift over the sports-focused establishment.

The walls are littered with memorabilia that means nothing to me. Sam loves sports and even played football this school year. They may interest my kid, but I still can't seem to get into them—not that it stops me from going to every single game and being the loudest mom on the sidelines.

I shift my gaze, doing another sweep in case River has arrived.

Nothing.

But what I do notice has my shoulders shrinking, and that familiar feeling of sadness hits me in the gut.

There are couples snuggled up in every corner.

One guy leans into a beautiful blonde, brushing his lips across her cheek and to her ear. She giggles, leaning into him and clutching his thigh.

Two guys sit with their heads together at a booth in the back, their smiles full of promises of what's to come.

I'm so damn destitute for romance of any kind, and jealousy and longing run through me.

I spent my formative years with the same man who got me pregnant at sixteen, Patrick, and we were together for eleven years. Though we've now been divorced for two, I haven't dated anyone since him. Haven't slept with anyone either. Hell, I haven't *kissed* anyone since him.

Lonely is my middle name at this point.

It could be hormones and all the stress of this apartment fiasco, but I've been extra miserable about the state of my love life—or lack thereof—since my two best friends have found that *once-in-a-lifetime* kind of love in the last six months.

I watch River and Dean bicker and argue—then make up within two minutes. Watch Caroline and Cooper, who have been best friends for a decade, stare at each other with nothing but hearts in their eyes.

I want that.

I want to know what it's like to be loved again. Want to feel what they're feeling, that rush when someone looks at you like you're their whole world. I miss being part of a couple. Miss all the cutesy shit and all the romantic gestures.

I want it again.

"Disgusting, isn't it?"

A deep voice startles me, and I glance at the now occupied stool next to me.

A guy is sitting there, staring out at the crowd, scanning it.

The first thing I notice is how tall he is. I'm not lacking in the height department, but even sitting down I can tell this guy is at least six inches taller than I am.

I tip my head back, peering up at his profile.

His jaw is strong and sharp, dusted with hair like he forgot to shave. There's a bump along his nose, like he's broken it before, and I have the strangest urge to ask him what happened. Ridiculous since I don't know him.

His inky black hair is tapered at the sides, longer on top and disheveled like he's run his hands through it several times. His focus is on the crowd, and I wonder if he was talking to me at all.

Then, he nods at the throng of people and leans into me. It's not enough that I'm uncomfortable, just enough so I can hear him…and smell him.

And damn does he smell good.

Like fresh mountain air with a hint of something minty.

"All the lovey-dovey shit," he says out of the side of his mouth, shaking his head. "It's a bit overrated if you ask me."

"Yet nobody did."

He pulls back, looking down at me for the first time.

My breath is caught in my throat when his eyes meet mine.

They're a bright, light blue. Maybe the brightest I've ever seen in person.

The color is striking against his long lashes, but it's not the only thing drawing me in.

He's looking at me like it's only us in the room. It's intense, and not how you should look at a stranger.

My skin prickles with goose bumps.

Finally, he flicks his eyes away.

I swallow, my mouth tacky and dry.

Oh hell. I need to get ahold of myself. Stop acting like I haven't seen an attractive man before. Sure, it's been a while since anyone other than Henry Cavill has given me tingles, but still. I need to get a grip.

"Ask you," I say to him, doing my best to ignore the way his stare has my pulse racing. "Nobody asked you."

A grin pulls at his full lips. "That's fair."

I smile back at him and spin around on the stool, facing the bar. The stranger copies my movements, and our elbows brush during the movement.

He doesn't miss the contact either, glancing down at where we touched before his eyes flit to mine again.

I'm embarrassed by the heat flowing through me.

I'm ridiculous. It's a damn elbow—but it's been *that* long since I've had any physical contact from an attractive man.

Pity.

He lifts his hand, flagging down the bartender, and it draws my attention. His hand is big, covered in small scratches, and his forearms are corded with muscle. A dark blue short-sleeved shirt stretches across his body when he moves. It's tight, but not in a *Hey, look at how much time I spend in the gym* kind of tight. Besides, I have a feeling his build isn't from time spent in the gym, but rather from whatever it is he does for a living.

The bartender saunters our way.

My lips pinch together in annoyance because he couldn't be bothered when I wanted a drink.

"Your usual?" he asks the stranger, never mind that I was here first.

I'm about to let him know he forgot about me when the mysterious man next to me speaks.

"Please, and whatever she's having."

I'm not dumb enough to argue about a free drink after the day—hell, weeks—I've had.

"I'll have a whiskey sour, light on the simple syrup," I tell the bartender. "I'd like to taste the *top-shelf* bourbon, please."

He grins, then nods and whirls around to grab our drinks.

"So we're clear," I say to the man next to me, "just because I'm letting you buy me a drink, it doesn't mean anything. I'm not going home with you."

He nods, fighting a grin. "Duly noted."

I tuck my lips together, combatting my own smile.

We sit together in silence. It's not comfortable, but it's not *un*comfortable either.

I like having him here next to me despite not knowing him.

"I tried flagging him down twice, you know," I say, breaking the quiet.

"Don't hold it against him. Donny's a good guy. He just

13

gets distracted sometimes." The stranger tips his head toward the other end of the bar. "Especially when his partner stops by."

I lean forward to get a glimpse. A man who looks strikingly like Taye Diggs, so much I half expect him to start singing about my rent, sits at the other end, chin resting in his hand. He's watching the bartender work with lustful eyes, and I'm jealous all over again.

"Is this some sort of couples bar?"

"Usually? No." He twists his neck around, looking at the room again. "I'm not sure what's in the air tonight."

"Do I detect disdain in your voice?"

He chuckles. "That obvious?"

"Yes. That and your opening comment really gave it away."

Donny pivots our way, drinks in his hands.

"A whiskey sour for the lady, top shelf." He slides my glass toward me, then sets the other in front of the stranger. "And neat scotch for Brooks."

Brooks.

The name fits him and doesn't all at the same time.

"Let me know when you're ready for refills," Donny says.

Brooks nods, picking his glass up and taking a sip. He doesn't grimace, doesn't shake his head after the burn like my ex-husband always did when he tried to drink hard liquor.

I like that he doesn't do that.

"I'm not some guy drowning his sorrows at a bar, all down on relationships because he's been broken up with, if that's what you're thinking."

It wasn't.

"Duly noted," I chirp back at him.

Another grin pulls at his lips. It's not a full smile, just a soft tug at his lips that's more mischievous than amused. Though I don't know him, I like it when he does it.

It's…cute.

Which isn't a fitting word for a guy as big as him.

"So, what has *you* here drowning your sorrows? Get broken up with?"

I snort. "Something like that."

I wasn't dumped in the traditional sense, but my landlord did basically break up with me.

It was just via an eviction notice.

"That bad, huh?"

"That bad." I gulp down a drink of my whiskey sour, grimacing as the liquor hits the back of my throat. Donny made up for ignoring me by adding extra alcohol.

Guess I can let Donny off the hook this time.

"I got an eviction notice."

I'm not sure why I tell him.

He's nobody to me. Has no business being privy to this embarrassing information.

But maybe that's why I say it.

"It's not a surprise. I've known about it for weeks. Just can't seem to get my crap together. But it hit me today that I'm going to be homeless in about three weeks if I can't find something between now and then. Saying it was a punch to the gut would be an understatement."

"Fuck. That *is* bad." He lifts his hand, signaling at Donny for a refill. He peeks back over at me. "You need another drink."

"Gentle reminder that my statement from before stands," I tell him, narrowing my eyes.

Those startling blue irises of his sparkle, and it's not only the grin lining his lips that's mischievous.

"That so?"

"That's so." I push my shoulders back, though I'm not sure even I believe it.

His eyes darken with a promise, and my breath is caught in my throat as he leans into me for the second time tonight. His lips are a short distance away. I've never had the urge to kiss a total stranger before, but right now?

Right now, I could kiss the hell out of him.

"Trust me, I have better moves to get you to go home with me than buying you drinks."

I had no intentions of coming out tonight to find a guy to go home with.

But the more sips of alcohol that burn my throat and the more this man stares at me like I'm the only thing he wants to see, the more my guard slips.

And the more the idea of going home with him doesn't sound so crazy after all.

Chapter 2

NOLAN

A bar is the last place I wanted to be tonight.

After hanging up my helmet for the day, I wasn't in the mood for company. Tired from getting up at the ass-crack of dawn, all I wanted was to go home. I had a six-pack of beer and leftover Chinese waiting for me in the fridge. My couch was calling my name, and a new true crime documentary awaited me.

But when your best friend calls and tells you you're going out...well, you're fucking going out.

Now that I'm here, I kind of wish I'd spent more time on my appearance, like running a comb through my hair instead of my fingers or shaving the stubble that's grown in since this morning.

It has everything to do with the girl sitting next to me.

I noticed her the moment I opened the door to Hole in One, a hidden gem this city has no idea it's missing out on.

She stared out at the crowd with sad eyes, but it wasn't the melancholy gaze that made her stand out. I mean, fuck, it's a bar—most people in a bar *are* sad.

Nah.

It was the way that, despite the sadness, she had her shoulders pressed back and sat upon the stool as if it were a throne.

Her thoughts consumed her so much I doubt she noticed she had the attention of several people, including me. Her pouty bottom lip was stuck between her teeth, and her brows pinched together in concentration.

I glanced at her finger—empty—and before I knew it, I was sitting next to her.

She spent at least another thirty seconds watching the crowd while I watched her.

I still don't know her name, but I do know she might be the most gorgeous girl I've ever seen in person.

Her deep brown hair hangs in waves down her back. My fingers itch to touch it. Just like I'm dying to lean into her and get a better smell of whatever perfume she's wearing, the one I keep catching a whiff of every time she shifts around.

Which she's doing right now.

She clears her throat and fits her hands around her *top-shelf* whiskey sour, pushing her shoulders back again, pretending my words did not affect her when they did. Her pink cheeks give her away.

I fight a smirk.

"It's not my fault," she informs me, like she's embarrassed I might think she's unable to pay her bills.

If that were the case, I'd be the last person to judge her.

I can't count the number of late notices we received growing up. My dad was a single parent raising a hellion of a kid in a down economy. We struggled, swam our way through debt and notice after notice.

She'll receive no judgment from me.

Hell, most of us are one bad day away from being on the shit end of a notice like that. It happens, and it's nothing to be ashamed of.

"The owner of the building sold the land, and they don't need to keep the apartments," she explains. "They have plans to tear everything down and replace it."

She can't be talking about…

"Who knew 7th Street was such an ideal location for an outdoor sports equipment store?"

Fuck me.

Donny slides two more glasses in front of us, and I could kiss the bastard for his timing.

I swallow down a good gulp, attempting to smash away the guilt pitching a tent in my chest.

The first time I go out in ages…

The first girl I meet in months…

And she lives in the building my boss bought and plans to tear down, meaning *I'm* part of the reason she's struggling right now.

Fucking awesome.

"It's fine though. I'll figure it out." She blows out a breath, picking up her new drink and shaking her head. "I always do."

"I'm sorry," I tell her, because I am.

"Not your fault."

Except it is.

She shrugs, taking a drink. Setting the glass down, she rolls her tongue across her plump lips, flicking away the hair that's fallen over her shoulder. "So, if you're not here drowning your sorrows—*allegedly*—then what brings you in?" She lifts a sculpted brow. "Let me guess, you're looking for love?"

Given my obvious displeasure with the number of couples here tonight, I know she's teasing.

I bark out a laugh. "Not a chance."

"And here I had you pegged for a Romeo."

"Only if you'll be my Juliet."

She cringes at the same time I do, and we laugh.

"That was awful, huh?"

"Very."

"I promise I have better lines than that."

She lifts her brows again. "I thought you weren't looking for love."

I pull a face at the mention of *love*, and she laughs.

"You not a believer in happily ever afters or something?"

Another swallow of scotch because I can't help the memories barreling through my mind.

I haven't always been so against the idea of forever with someone. I remember the days when my parents would dance in the kitchen and my mother would smile up at my father with pure adoration. Even then I thought, *I want that.*

Then, life as I knew it was ripped away one snowy December day.

My mom told my dad she'd met someone else who would love her like she wanted to be loved, packed her bags, and left.

For years, I watched my father nurse his heartbreak. Watched him try to figure out where it all went wrong.

He never did, and he died five years ago with a broken heart.

I refuse to ever let someone have that much power over

me, and I avoid relationships like the plague. Building a relationship with someone means giving them the ability to hurt you, and I'll pass on that. I'm fine with keeping things casual. No need to get emotions involved.

I repeat her words from earlier back to her. "Something like that." Though, unlike her, I have no intentions of divulging any more information.

Luckily, she doesn't press.

"My best friend forced me out," I tell her instead. "Except he's running late."

"Mine too! The brat had the audacity to text me to brag why she's running late." I pick up on what she's referring to as she sighs, the frustration clear in the way her shoulders set inward. "Whatever. I'm not complaining about her forcing me to hang out though." She shrugs. "I could use the drinks and distraction."

"Because of the eviction."

Eviction.

The word tastes bitter on my tongue.

I've never thought much about my job and the buildings my boss buys to tear down and rebuild. I just show up at the jobsite, get the work done, and collect my paycheck.

Meeting someone whose life is getting flipped around so my already loaded boss can pad his pocket some more?

It fucking sucks the life out of me.

I went through something similar at the end of last year. The owner of the tiny-as-hell studio apartment I'd been renting for years passed away, and the kids opted to sell the property. The sale happened so fast, in the end I only had about two weeks to find a new place and move.

Thanks to a good word from Dean, I was able to score the

open apartment in his building. It's more expensive than I wanted it to be, but the neighbor—and living space—is a massive upgrade for which I was long overdue. Luckily, I have solid savings to get me through until I can find a roommate or two.

She lifts her whiskey sour into the air. "To my liver, the real MVP of the night!"

"Though I believe I deserve the title for being the one providing the drinks for your liver, I'll allow it."

"I wasn't finished." She lifts the glass higher. "And to the handsome stranger who's taking pity on me!"

She giggles, and I toss back the rest of my scotch in solidarity...and because I could use the drink myself.

I've been up since four thirty this morning and was on the jobsite by five. Then I had to listen to my co-workers complain for ten hours about how much they hate their wives and children.

Dean's lucky as hell he's like a brother, or else I'd have turned him down when he texted.

"You think I'm handsome?"

She pins me with a stare that says *Don't play dumb,* then lifts her glass again.

She swallows down another healthy drink and rolls her tongue over her lips.

I try not to pay attention to the way my jeans tighten in areas they should *not* be tightening in.

But I shouldn't be surprised. It's been way too fucking long since I've been with someone. I could use a little relief between the sheets.

I flag Donny down, signaling for another drink before I let my thoughts wander too far. He knows me well enough to know I'll be switching to beer for the rest of the night, so I'm not surprised when he reaches for a bottle of my favorite local brew.

He scuttles our way, dropping the bottle in front of me and taking my empty tumbler.

"Are you ready for another?" I ask, nodding toward her dwindling drink. They're small glasses, so I'm not surprised she's almost out again.

She tilts her head. "I should inform you you're not coming home with me either, *Romeo*."

I grin at the nickname. I should probably tell her my real one, but why offer up information she's not willing to give too?

"I'm not trying to get you to go home with me...yet." I smirk. "Just being a gentleman." *And trying to ease my guilt...*

She nods, accepting that. "I'll have one more, please," she says to Donny.

"Coming right up." He scurries off to grab her drink.

She rests an elbow on the bar, pinning me with those mysterious gray eyes of hers. "Why *are* you buying me drinks then?"

Straightforward.

I like that too.

I decide to give her the same treatment.

"Well, the first was because I felt bad for you given your situation. Plus"—I drag my eyes down her body, then back to her face—"have you seen your legs in those jeans?"

She smiles at the compliment, and I like that she takes it at face value. Too many times have I tried to compliment a woman and had her try to talk me out of it. I like a confident woman.

"No other motives?"

"Well…" I exhale slowly, then grimace. "My boss is the one who bought your building."

She inhales a sharp breath, eyes widening at the confession.

I don't know her well enough to be able to tell if she's mad or just shocked, but she's quiet as she stares at me with a look I'm unfamiliar with.

Donny breaks her concentration as he sets the replenished drink in front of her.

Her eyes narrow to slits. "Guess that makes us enemies, then."

"Afraid so."

"So these are guilt drinks?"

"Yes and no. I'm hoping they'd help my chances if I were to ask you if you want to go out sometime."

"Sometime?"

"Sometime." I shrug, deciding to show all my cards. "Or tonight. Your call."

A grin curls the corners of her lips upward, and I can tell that, despite her earlier claims, she likes the idea. "Is that so?"

"Yes."

"Then ask me."

My eyes are drawn to her exposed shoulder as she sets her chin in her hand, leaning onto the bar, waiting.

I have the strangest urge to lean down and kiss it.

Since when did shoulders become sexy?

Her gray eyes are lit with anticipation, and I hear the hitch in her breath when I bend toward her.

Despite her insistence on not going home with me, I have no doubt if I were to ask, she'd say yes.

"Tell me your name and I'll ask you anything you want."

She expels the breath she was holding on a short laugh, giving me a flirty smile. "I thought we'd settled on Juliet."

"Is that what we're going to do? Play pretend?"

It would be the first time I've done that with a girl.

But something tells me she's not one for games.

"I—"

Her phone buzzes against the counter, dragging us both away from the moment as she shoves her hand into her purse.

She looks at the screen and frowns.

"I'm sorry," she says, not glancing up. "I have to take this."

She grabs her purse and rushes through the bar toward the bathrooms.

If I hadn't watched her face fall with worry, I'd have assumed this was a gimmick to get out of telling me her name.

Now I'm just concerned and hoping she's okay.

"You scare her off already?" Donny asks.

I stare after her. "I hope not."

Because I fully intend to continue the conversation when she returns.

She's standing just inside the short hallway; I can see her from my vantage point.

Her eyes widen, then a bright smile transforms her face.

It's different from the smiles she's been giving me, and I find myself a little jealous of whoever is on the phone.

Which is ridiculous considering I still don't know her name.

"Dude!" A heavy hand lands on my shoulder, and I pivot toward the familiar voice. "Sorry we're late. We got a little…occupied."

The proud smirk on my best friend's face transforms into a twist of pain when his girlfriend smacks him in the stomach.

"Dean!" she hisses, crossing her arms over her chest. "Can you not?"

"I could, but what's the fun in that?"

"Ignore him." She rolls her eyes, pretending to be annoyed by him. "Hi, Nolan."

"Hey, River." I smile at her, loving how she can go from evil to sweet as pie at a moment's notice. She keeps Dean on his toes, that's for sure. "How's shit?"

She laughs at my phrasing. "Shit's fine. Just trying to keep this idiot in line." She hooks her thumb over her shoulder toward Dean. "I don't know how you've put up with him all these years."

"Excuse me," he says. "I'm charming as fuck."

"Charming is *not* the word I'd use for you."

I agree, and I can say that since I've known him since we met at the bus stop in kindergarten.

"This place is busy." River hops onto the abandoned stool, glancing around the bar. "I'm not seeing Maya anywhere. I texted her to let her know we're here."

"She's probably in the bathroom. That woman has the worst bladder ever."

At the mention of the bathrooms, I glance toward the hallway.

It's empty.

She left.

My shoulders sag in disappointment.

I don't know who she is or if I'll ever see her again, but I have a feeling those gray eyes are going to haunt me.

"Speaking of...I gotta hit the head. Then I'll find us a table."

"You try pushing a child from your vagina and see how your bladder holds up!"

The a-little-too-loud words River yells at Dean's back draw my attention.

"Do I finally get to meet the elusive Maya?" I ask her.

River and Dean have been dating several months now, and I've yet to meet the best friend River never shuts up about. I've met her kid already during a game of pickup with Dean, but not her. Our schedules haven't lined up yet.

I'm curious as hell to meet the woman who has been able to deal with River for the last twenty years. The girl is a handful on a good day.

River bobs her head. "Yep. I managed to coax her out of her crappy little apartment. She needs to spend the night away from all the moving stress."

"She's moving? Away from here?"

"No, just apartments. Her—" Her phone buzzes in her hand, drawing her attention. "Ah, she was in the bathroom. Oooh, this is interesting."

"What is?"

River holds her phone against her chest, hiding it from me like I'm going to peer down and read the screen. "Nothing."

"Look who I found coming out of the shitters," Dean says, sliding back up to us.

River pins him with a glare. "Did you leave your manners at home?"

"Stop acting like you hate my dirty mouth. I have fresh scratches on my back to prove otherwise."

Her back snaps straight, eyes widening in horror. "Dean Evans!"

"I'm just saying…" He shrugs. "Anyway, Nolan, this is Maya. Maya, meet the second most handsome man in the bar tonight."

He moves out of the way, and my stomach drops.

It's *her*.

Her eyes widen. Jaw drops.

I can't believe my fucking luck today.

"Hi."

The single word comes out a whisper, and all I manage to do is stare at her like a dolt.

It's a different stare than earlier.

This one is full of disbelief.

It wouldn't have mattered if I'd asked her out or what her answer would have been. It never mattered.

She's completely off limits.

Not because she's River's best friend.

No.

Maya comes with attachments, and I don't do attachments.

She's the first to break eye contact, and fuck am I thankful for it.

I clear my throat, rising to my feet. I hold my hand out to her. "Sorry, I guess Dean's not the only one with bad manners tonight. It's nice to finally meet you, *Maya*."

Her brows rise at the inflection, and she pastes on a fake smile.

"Yeah, good to meet you too, *Nolan*."

You lied is what she's really saying with her eyes as she slides her hand into mine.

I didn't lie, you assumed is what mine say back, working

hard as fuck to ignore the way her hand feels against mine. It's soft and tiny compared to my mitt. I hold on a beat longer than I should, hoping no one notices.

"I spotted a table over that way." Dean points behind him. "How about you ladies go grab it and Nolan and I can handle the drinks?"

They practically run away from us, probably wanting some girl time together.

"So, uh, that's Maya," he says once they're out of earshot.

"Yeah, man, kinda gathered that."

He trains his eyes on me, studying me hard.

I hate the way he's looking at me. Staring at me like I'm not telling him something.

Which, to be fair, I'm not. But he doesn't know that.

I ignore him, lifting my hand for Donny. Man, I'm going to owe him one hell of a tip tonight.

Fortunately, Donny isn't busy, so he rushes right over, not allowing any time for Dean to start peppering me with questions.

"Another round?" Donny points at my beer.

I nod, paying no attention to the stare Dean's still burning into me.

"For you, Dean? Your usual beer?"

"Please, and whatever rye-heavy bourbon you have, too. Neat."

"Didn't take either of your ladies as bourbon girls." He taps the counter once. "Coming right up."

I hold my breath as Donny walks away, knowing what's coming from Dean before he says it.

"What the hell was that?" he demands.

I play it cool, picking at the label on my beer bottle.

29

"What was what?" I ask, as if I have no idea what he's talking about.

He pins me with a *Don't bullshit me* stare.

I sigh.

"It was nothing."

"Right. Very convincing, Brooks."

He says my last name like a cuss word. He only calls me Brooks when he's annoyed with me.

I don't have the mental capacity to deal with it right now.

"Here you go." Donny slides River's and Maya's drinks toward us. "Let me grab your beers."

Dean's eyes are trained on the two drinks sitting in front of us.

"Sure fucking looks like nothing," Dean mutters.

He's well aware I only ordered one.

He's wondering how Donny knows what Maya was drinking.

Donny sets our bottles down, and I tell him to put them on my tab.

Dean pushes away from the counter, his and River's drinks in his hands.

With a sigh, I follow him.

This night just got a hell of a lot more interesting.

Chapter 3

MAYA

"So what happened to the hottie?" River asks the moment we're alone. "Did you get his number?"

I shot off a text to her in the bathroom telling her about the hot guy I met and how I had every intention of getting his number. What I didn't mention is if my kid hadn't called to interrupt us, I'd have gone home with Nolan tonight.

Nolan who is Brooks.

Dean's best friend.

Just my luck that the first guy who so much as glances my way since my divorce ends up being *completely* off limits.

"Nah," I tell her. "He was gone by the time I got out of the bathroom."

She frowns. "Boo. Men suck."

She launches into a story about something that happened with a customer at the boutique today. I should be paying attention since I'm an investor and employee of said store, but I can't.

My mind is running a mile a minute thinking of all the

ways this night almost went to hell because I was going to be impulsive for the first time in forever.

I should have known better.

The last time I was impulsive, I lost my virginity in the back seat of a rusty Grand Marquis.

I got zero orgasms and pregnant.

"Ha! I knew it!" River says, setting her phone back down on the table.

Her excitement draws my attention.

"Caroline?" I ask.

"Yep. She and Cooper are going to stay in tonight."

She bounces her brows up and down, and jealousy zings through me again.

"Good grief. Is everyone getting laid except me?"

"Afraid so. I'd be more than happy to help find you someone to date. Or hook up with. Dating isn't all it's cracked up to be, you know."

"Says the woman with the perfect boyfriend."

She doesn't bother hiding the lovesick smile on her face.

I glare at her. "Stop rubbing it in."

"Sorry, not sorry." She tosses her long, deep red hair over her shoulder. "Anyway, how's my nephew doing?"

"Oddly enough, I'd just gotten off the phone with him when you arrived."

"Oh crap. What'd the little shit do now? Burn the mac and cheese again?"

"No, thank god." I shudder, still able to recall the smell of the burnt noodles. "But guess who didn't show up again?"

She pulls a face. "Ugh, seriously?"

Patrick's parenting style is similar to how he handled our marriage. He's not a bad father, but he's not the most attentive one either. Oftentimes his work gets priority over Sam, which is what happened tonight. He got a last-minute project from a client, has to fly out in the morning, and won't be back until Wednesday.

I tell River this and she tsks. "Of course. Work first, offspring second."

Part of me wants to laugh because River is as bad as Patrick when it comes to work sometimes.

Then again, she doesn't have a child at home who needs her love and attention.

"Anyway, to make up for it, Patrick got some suite tickets to a hockey game. It's Thursday and he wanted to check with me before he told his dad *yes* so my feelings weren't hurt about him spending a day with his dad during my week."

"Aww." River clutches her chest. "Sometimes he can be so sweet."

I grin, proud of the young man I'm raising.

I remember when I found out I was pregnant at sixteen. I still remember the way my hands shook as I held the pregnancy test, terrified of what the future held for me and my unborn baby.

Now, here I am thirteen years later, and I'm just as scared, just as worried about the future, only for different reasons.

"He can be. But I worry he's going to think his dad is cooler than me because he can afford all the fun extra stuff."

Although Patrick pays his fair share of child support, bills still stack up sometimes and I don't always have the extra cash to throw into savings for those expenses that pop up out of nowhere…like being forced to move out of my apartment.

Plus, I'm more conservative with my money than Patrick is.

His family didn't disown him when he got me pregnant. Mine did. I know what it's like to lose that security blanket, and I don't want that to ever happen again.

"Sam thinks you hung the moon," she assures me. "You don't have to worry about that at all."

"He *has* to love me. I'm his mom and provide a roof over his head."

"Speaking of…did you ever hear back on the apartment you had the lead on?"

I sink my teeth into my bottom lip, reminded of the email I got today.

My non-answer is answer enough, and the pity is back in River's eyes. It's the one thing I can't stand, especially from her.

"Oh, Maya." She blows out a heavy breath. "I'm so sorry."

"I'll figure it out." I wave her off. "If I need to, I'll call Patrick and he'll help us out. I—"

"No way!" She shakes her head. "And give the jerk the satisfaction? Hell no. We'll figure something out."

We'll.

She says it like we're a team, and I guess that's because we are.

I smile, and tears sting my eyes for the second time tonight.

Of course she has my back. She always does.

"I'll put more feelers out. Maybe Darlene at The Gravy Train knows someone who's looking for a tenant or a roommate." I cringe at the word *roommate*, and she holds her hand up. "I know, I know. Having a roommate isn't the ideal situation with Sam. But, if it's your only option until you can find *something* better, it is what it is, you know?" She snaps her fingers. "Oh! I just had a crazy thought."

"What?"

"Nolan."

My heart jumps into my throat at the mention of him.

I can't get the way he looked at me out of my mind. It was the kind of stare a girl could get used to, and I can't afford to get used to it.

"What about him?"

"He's looking for a room——"

She doesn't get the full word out before I'm shaking my head.

"Absolutely not," I say.

"But——"

I pin her with the same stare I do Sam when he's attempting to argue his way out of—or into—something. "No buts. It's a no."

"Why not? Because he's hot?"

Don't react. Don't react. Do not *react.*

"Because he's a stranger."

"True, but Dean and I can both vouch for him. Besides, it's not permanent. It's just until you hear back about your other applications."

She has a point there…

But there's no way I could live with Nolan.

I don't know him. Sam doesn't know him.

I can't uproot my kid and move him into some random guy's apartment because I suck at being an adult.

Especially when the guy made me squirm one too many times in such a short amount of time.

35

"No." The word is final, maybe a little too sharp. "Please drop it."

Her mouth floats open again, then she snaps it shut. She's not mad, that much I can tell, and I know she wants to say something else.

I just don't want to hear it.

"It's dropped." She grins. "Just let me know if I need to kick Dean out to the couch."

She would, too, and as much as the idea pains me, staying with River might be the only choice I have in the end. But I refuse to accept her offer until I've run out of all my other options.

I don't want to be anyone's burden.

"Why am I sleeping on the couch now?" Dean slips a neat bourbon in front of River and takes the seat next to her.

She leans over and presses a quick kiss to his cheek in thanks.

I realize in this moment that Nolan has nowhere to sit but next to me.

My heart hammers in my chest, so hard I can hear it in my ears.

Ridiculous since I just spent quite a while sitting next to him flirting.

He slides another whiskey sour in front of me as he drops onto the stool next to me, and I give him a small smile.

But he doesn't see it. He refuses to look at me.

"How'd you know Maya loves whiskey sours?" River questions him.

He lifts his big shoulders. "Who doesn't love a whiskey sour?"

Dean coughs out a laugh, and Nolan looks the other way.

Huh.

"So, the couch?"

River glances at me, then at Nolan. She's asking for permission to share what's going on.

She has no idea it's pointless because Nolan knew before her anyway.

I nod.

"Maya's lead fell through."

"What?" Dean's beautiful green eyes widen, and he runs a hand over his face. "Dude, that sucks. I'm…shit." He shakes his head. "You know you're more than welcome to stay at our place. I'm sure we can make it work."

I adore him for the offer, but we both know it'll never work, especially since I have no idea how long I'd be crashing there.

"Thanks, Dean. You're not as bad as River says you are."

"All her smack talk about me is just foreplay."

I laugh because he's not wrong.

River and Dean fight more than anyone I've ever met, but they're so in love it's almost sickening sometimes.

"What are you going to do?" he asks.

"Pray?" I laugh, though there's no humor to it. Then I shrug. "I have several applications out—and have had them out for a couple weeks—but no bites yet. Finding something within the price range I have and within the school district is hard. I was lucky I even found my current apartment."

Nolan shifts beside me, and I'm sure it's because he's feeling guilty about being part of the company that bought the building.

The guilt isn't his to carry. It's business, not a personal vendetta.

If anything, I find it comical it's him.

And I mean comical in a way that is not funny at all.

It's sort of the theme of my life. Nothing has gone the way I planned since the moment I found out I was pregnant at sixteen.

Well, that's not entirely true. I knew my parents would kick me out of the house, and that's exactly what they did. I can count on two hands the number of times I've seen them since I had Sam.

But before that, River and I had our whole lives planned out.

We were supposed to graduate high school and attend college here in Colorado. She was going for her degree in business, and I was eager to take as many classes as I could my freshman year to see what sparked my joy. We'd get an apartment in the city and live together throughout school. I wanted to date around, wanted to party my ass off. I was ready to create memories I'd never forget.

Except college never came.

I was too busy at home taking care of a baby who wouldn't stop crying while my husband—we got married shortly after I turned eighteen—worked at his dad's consulting firm.

Life hasn't been the same since I was sixteen, and despite where I am right now, worrying about where I'm going to live, I wouldn't change a damn thing about it.

I got Sam.

He's all I need.

Everything else will fall into place.

"So," River says, breaking the tension that has settled over the group, "how are you liking your new apartment, Nolan?"

I snap my head toward her, pinning her with my heated stare because this is *not* dropping it.

She doesn't look at me because she knows what she's doing is wrong.

"It's nice," Nolan answers. "Quiet compared to my last place."

Dean huffs. "You aren't lying about that."

"It wasn't *that* bad."

"Trust me, it was. The couple next door fought all the time, and the cops were always tailing the neighbor."

"Sorry, not all of us are used to the life of luxury, rich boy."

Dean flips him off, but there's no ire behind it.

I almost forget sometimes that Dean's family is loaded. They grew up on the poorer end but ended up hitting the jackpot—*literally*.

He doesn't live off his family's money, choosing to support himself off his teacher's salary. I admire him for it. He's doing what he loves and doesn't care what his family thinks of him. Having gone through what I did with my own family and doing the opposite of what they wanted me to do —like keeping my baby—I can relate.

"Well, either way," River says, "we're glad to have you in the building. Now when Dean's being annoying, I can send him up to your floor."

"No fucking way." Nolan shakes his head. "I've dealt with his ass since we were kids. He's your problem now."

"Don't remind me," she complains.

Dean leans his head on her shoulder. "You know you love me."

"Only sometimes." She kisses his forehead.

"Disgusting," Nolan mutters.

"Amen."

He glances over at me, and it's the first time our eyes have met since he sat down.

His bright blue gaze pierces me with the same intensity as before, and I hope nobody else can hear the way my breathing kicks up a notch. I want to say something, ask him if he knew who I was.

But I don't get the chance.

"So, Maya, is Sam still interested in baseball this summer?"

River's question pulls us from the moment, and Nolan's the first to break the stare.

"He is. But that may change after the game Thursday."

"The Storm game?"

"Yes, Patrick's taking him."

"He got a suite." River rolls her eyes as she says it, annoyed by how flashy Patrick is on my behalf. "Probably got it through his daddy."

Or he could have done it himself. He certainly has the connections. Some of his clients are making more money a year than I could ever hope to see in a lifetime.

It's crazy some days to think I went from a four-bedroom house with a two-car garage and a brand-new SUV every year to almost on the verge of couch-surfing in two years.

I might not have the house or a fancy new car—both my choices—but getting out of my loveless marriage was worth it. By the time we decided to get divorced, I couldn't remember the last time Patrick and I had so much as kissed.

"A suite?" Dean's brows fly up. "Remind me, Maya, how

friendly are you and Patrick again? Could he, say, score *me* some tickets?"

"Dean!" River swats at him.

"What?" He dodges her assault. "It's just a question! I'm not asking her to sleep with him again. Just get a few tickets to a hockey game."

River huffs. "Ignore him."

I laugh. "Thank god for that. Been there, done that. Got the mediocre sex badge to prove it."

Nolan grunts beside me, and I ignore him.

"Oh! Shit!" Dean slaps the table, then points across from him. "Why the fuck didn't I think of this before?"

"What?" River asks. "What's going on?"

"Nolan!"

"That'd be my name," he drawls, fingering the label on his beer bottle.

"You have rooms. You were telling me yesterday how you were looking for roommates."

"I'm curious how the mention of shitty sex reminded you of me, but yes, I do."

"Mediocre," I correct.

He glances over at me. "There's no such thing as mediocre sex. It's either shitty or it's not. There's no in-between."

"This is perfect," Dean rambles on. "Maya can move in and help cover the rent while you go through the vetting process of finding someone. It's a total win-win."

I don't say anything.

I'm not sure what Dean's version of win-win is, but mine doesn't include moving my son and myself in with a guy I just met.

"Plus, you'll be living in my building. Which, if you ask

41

me, is the biggest advantage of all this," River adds with a megawatt grin.

I narrow my eyes at her, frustrated as hell.

To her credit, she doesn't shrink away.

"While *I* appreciate both of you trying to find me a place to stay, I don't think Nolan appreciates you offering up his apartment to a stranger."

Nolan clears his throat and shifts beside me again, appearing as uncomfortable with the idea as I am.

I wonder if it's for the same reasons as me.

"Actually, it's not a bad idea."

My jaw drops.

I didn't hear him right.

There is *no* way I heard him right.

"What?"

He shrugs. "Dean's right. I do need a roommate to help cover the rent. I have savings I've been digging into until I could find someone, and, well, savings ain't savings if I'm spending it, right?"

"You're serious?"

He tips his head. "Why are you surprised by that?"

"Because we don't know each other."

His brow rises just the slightest bit. "I highly doubt you're going to murder me in my sleep."

"What if you murder *me* in *my* sleep?"

"Nah." He shakes his head. "Don't want the hassle."

"Not you don't want to murder me, just you don't want the hassle?"

River raises her hand. "I, too, have a problem with that statement, Nolan."

He chuckles, then points to Dean. "I've been best friends

with this idiot for the last two-plus decades. If I haven't murdered him yet, you're safe."

"I can't even be upset by that statement." Dean lifts his beer to his lips, taking a swig. "So, we're all set? Maya can move in?"

Nolan nods. "If she wants it, she can have the room."

"I have a son."

"Yeah, I heard. I also heard he got some pretty sweet tickets to a hockey game from his dad who is shitty at sex."

River snickers, and Dean almost spits his beer out.

I ignore them, narrowing my eyes at Nolan.

"Where would he sleep?"

"I imagine the other bedroom I have."

My brows crush together. "You have a three-bedroom apartment?"

Another nod. "I do."

"Why?"

"You're asking a lot of questions…"

"Just trying to get to know my potential roommate." I give him a saccharine smile.

His lips quirk upward. "Because it was the only thing available when the owner of my previous place died. Dean put in a good word with his building manager, and she got me into the first available unit."

"What the hell, Dean?" I glare at him. "Why didn't you put in a good word for me with Lucy?"

"Because you weren't homeless then!"

"If it makes you feel any better, I would have put in a good word for you. I'd much rather have you living there than Nolan." River smiles at him, lifting her glass to her lips. "No offense, Nolan."

"That is *highly* offensive," he argues.

She shrugs, swallowing a drink of her bourbon.

"I also take offense to that," Dean tells her. "You're implying your best friend is somehow better than my best friend."

They continue to argue, moving their attention to fighting over whose best friend deserves the apartment more like we aren't sitting here and hearing every word.

I mean, I'm not listening. I'm too busy freaking out.

I can't believe this is happening.

A few hours ago I thought I'd end up having to go to my ex-husband for help, and now here's a random, sexy-as-sin stranger offering to fix all my problems.

Okay, fine.

He's not random.

He's Dean's best friend.

But *I* don't know him. Sam doesn't really know him either.

It's only temporary...

Neither River nor Dean would get me into a sticky situation. They wouldn't have brought it up if they didn't both trust Nolan one hundred percent.

In all honesty, he doesn't give me any creeper vibes.

Well, at least as far as I can tell since I've only known him less than two hours.

What the hell am I thinking? I can't live with a stranger! Am I this desperate?

I hate that the answer is yes.

I *am* that desperate.

I need a place to stay, and right now, with four rejections

already, it's looking like I'm not going to be getting into any of the six places I've applied for.

But I'm still not sure…

There's a tap against my leg, and I glance up at Nolan.

"I meant what I said."

"Nolan…" I roll my tongue across my suddenly dry lips. He's looking at me like he's never been more serious about anything else before.

"Thought it was Romeo," he says in a hushed whisper, so soft I can hardly hear him.

"You know Romeo dies in the end, right?"

"Is that a threat?"

"Nah. Don't want the hassle."

He fights a grin, appreciating my callback. "There's no pressure to say yes, but the offer stands until I can find someone else."

I give him a simple nod.

For one of the first times in my life, I'm speechless… because I'm thinking of saying yes.

Chapter 4

Scotch has never betrayed me in my life, but I think it's what's to blame for my actions a few nights ago. It had to have lowered my sense of awareness of the words that came out of my mouth.

I told a woman she could move in with me.

A woman I don't really know.

A woman who has a kid.

I admit, some of it was because I felt guilty about being part of the reason she's about to be without a place to live.

Also, I felt bad for her.

I might be closed off in many ways, but it doesn't mean I don't have a heart somewhere in my icy chest. Since I was raised by one, the block of frigidness is a lot less thick when it comes to single parents.

I couldn't sit there knowing I have two perfectly good rooms that aren't being used while River's best friend is suffering.

Well, *one* of them is being used to house my book collection.

But I can clean it up and the kid can use it in the meantime.

Kid.

Fuck. I never in my wildest dreams thought I'd have a kid living with me.

They aren't really my forte.

They're too loud. Too messy. Full of too much attitude half the time. How Dean deals with the little shits all day long is beyond me.

Shit. Maybe Maya should take the library instead of her son…

But I guess I shouldn't worry about it until Maya accepts my offer.

When we parted ways Friday night, we exchanged numbers just in case. It's now Monday, and I haven't heard anything from her.

I'm betting she's too stubborn to take me up on it. She put off that vibe loud and clear at the bar.

It'd be a weird situation since we hardly know one another, but what other choice does she have at this point? I can imagine asking that many people to move out of an apartment building in a town already hurting for housing created quite the pickle for many. Being a single mom on a budget lessens her options even more.

Like it has happened several times over the last few days any time I've thought of her, images of her sultry smirk and those incredible gray eyes assault me.

That long hair made for pulling.

Those jeans that were painted onto her curves.

Those—

"Yo, Brooks, we're grabbing lunch. You in?"

47

"Huh?" I let my finger off the trigger of my welder and swing around to my co-worker, Jake, then push my face shield up and remove the respirator I always wear. "What's up?"

Jake is probably one of my closest friends outside of Dean…which is kind of sad when I think about it because we've only hung out outside of work a handful of times in the five years I've worked with him.

"Man, you must have really been zoning out. We tried to get your attention twice."

"Sorry, Jake. Just tired." After getting an early start yesterday morning, I stayed up too late last night watching some true crime documentary I couldn't shut off.

"Totally get it. We were wanting to know if you want to grab some lunch."

"Where are you guys going?"

"Gonna hit up that diner around the corner."

"The Gravy Train?"

He nods. "Yep. You in?"

Oftentimes I'm the guy who sits in the bed of his truck with a book and a sandwich, ignoring the rest of the world. But hearing the word *gravy* has my stomach rumbling for something better than two slices of bread and meat slapped together.

Jake chuckles. "I heard that shit from here, so I'll take that as a yes."

I pull my gloves off, tucking them into my pocket. "Meet you guys there?"

He nods. "Sounds good."

I finish cleaning up my area, knowing better than to leave my equipment lying around even if the area is monitored by security.

I learned a long-ass time ago not to trust anyone, especially the ones you're supposed to trust.

I toss my tools into the back seat of my truck, then strip off my heat-resistant jacket and exchange it for a dark blue flannel before climbing into the driver's seat.

It's a quick drive to the diner, and I'm pulling into the small public parking lot up the block no less than ten minutes later. I hop out and make my way along the street to the old train depot turned popular diner.

The Gravy Train is one of the best places in the whole city, and everyone knows it. Hell, even when I lived on the outskirts of town, I'd come here at least once a week to grab a slice of the pies they're famous for.

With me living so close now, my trips are admittedly more frequent.

I pull open the door and something smacks right into my chest.

No. Not something.

Some*one*.

Followed closely by a freezing liquid soaking into my flannel.

"Oh crap!" comes a soft voice. "I'm so sorry. I wasn't watching where I was going." The woman juggles the tray of coffees, then dips her head, reaching into her purse. She produces a huge wad of napkins and starts pressing them to the mess. "I'm such a klutz. I—Nolan?"

Maya.

She steps back, tilting her head up to get a better look at me.

Fucking hell.

I'd hoped the next time I saw her, she wasn't going to be as pretty as I remembered.

But fuck me if she isn't even more gorgeous than before.

She's peering up at me with her alarming gray eyes, and her dark lashes look even longer than they did the other night. If I'm not mistaken, there's a mix of surprise and pleasure in her gaze.

"Wha… What are you doing here?" She peeks around like she's searching for someone else. She wets her rosy pink bottom lip with her tongue. "Are you following me?"

I lift a brow as my lips curl into a smirk. "Uh, no. I'm not following you."

She doesn't appear to believe me.

"Lunch break." I hitch my thumb over my shoulder. "My jobsite is a few miles up the road. The guys wanted to come here, and I'm not dumb enough to say no to hot food in this weather."

She nods, shoving the napkins back into her purse. "It is really cold."

I point at the tray in her hand. "So cold you're drinking an iced coffee?"

She shrugs. "What? Sometimes you crave an iced coffee."

"Can't say I ever have."

Another nod, and a quiet falls over us, both unsure what to say next. She adjusts the tipped cup on the tray, then stares at the ground.

I stare at her, committing her curves to memory like the asshole I am.

She's wearing another pair of skintight jeans and booties, this time with a blue and white sweater that's striped across her middle and her arms. Her brown hair is hanging in waves down her back, and there's an adorable-as-fuck beanie with a puff sitting atop her head. Her cheeks are tinged pink, and I don't know if it's from the weather or her embarrassment.

"So, uh, you work around here?"

I drag my eyes back up to hers. If she caught me staring, she doesn't say so.

"This week, yeah."

"What do you do exactly? You know, besides knock down perfectly good apartment buildings."

I tuck my lips together, fighting a smile, because I doubt she'd appreciate that right now. "I'm a welder."

"Oh."

She falls quiet again, her brows drawing together.

I'm not sure why she says it like she does, but I don't bother asking.

I glance into the diner, noting the guys are all staring out at Maya like they've never seen a woman before.

A surge of protectiveness rumbles through my chest, and I glare at them.

"Well," Maya says, pulling my attention back to her. "I, uh, better get back to the shop." She lifts the coffees. "The girls are probably wondering where I am."

"You work with River, right?"

"Yep. Making Waves is right up the street." She inclines her head, indicating it's behind me. "We're right on the corner. We're closed on Mondays, but we're doing inventory today."

I don't tell her I know where it is.

Before River and Dean started dating, he used to pop in there for his mom and sister on their birthdays or for

Christmas. He'd deny it, but it was his way of supporting River because he had a huge crush on her.

I'd usually run up to The Gravy Train for coffee while he did his shopping because there was nothing of interest to me in there.

Well, at least I didn't think there was…until now.

"I…I'm sorry about the mess." She winces, noticing the wet spot on my shirt.

I shrug. "No big deal. I get messier than this most days."

"Right." She clears her throat. "Well, goodbye, Nolan."

I move out of her way as she steps around me.

She hustles down the street, and I stand there like an idiot watching her go.

It takes all of ten seconds for my brain to catch up.

"Maya! Wait!"

She swivels around, and I jog the short distance to her.

"Yeah?"

I shove my hands in my pockets, feeling nervous standing in front of her as she stares at me with questioning eyes.

"You, uh, you never called."

Her brows pinch together again.

"About the rooms," I remind her. "You haven't called."

"Oh." She sinks her teeth into her bottom lip. "I…I'm still not sure it's the best idea."

I'm not certain if it's relief or disappointment settling into my chest.

"It's not you," she rushes out. "It's just…"

She trails off, but I get what she's meaning.

I get it. It's a weird situation to be in.

"You don't need to explain. Just wanted you to know—"

"The offer still stands." She gives me a small smile, the first one I've gotten. "I know. Thank you."

"Of course." I nod. "I guess I'll see you around."

"You too…Romeo."

She turns, leaving me standing there staring at her for the second time.

"Who was that?" Jake asks as soon as I enter the diner and join him in line.

"Nobody."

"Can't remember the last time I looked at a nobody like that." He chortles, then claps me on the back.

Me either.

With a heavy sigh, I lean against the back wall of the elevator. I cross my arms over my chest and close my eyes as I relax into the space.

It's five thirty PM, and I've been up since five this morning.

After a shit night of sleep and a full day on the jobsite, I'm fucking beat.

"Hold the door!"

I don't move to press the button.

Not because I'm being a dick, but because I'm *that* tired.

A hand slips between the twin doors just as they're about to close.

Dean slides into the elevator car with a hard stare directed my way.

"Hey, fucker. I said hold the door." He shakes his head, taking up a post next to me. He leans one foot against the wall and tilts his head back, looking up at the ceiling. "How come nobody in this damn apartment building can hold the door for people?"

"Probably because nobody wants to share an elevator with you."

"You kidding? They only wish they could be so lucky. You look like shit, by the way."

I loll my head his way. "Careful, Dean. You keep sweet-talking like that and I might start to suspect you're crushing on me."

He huffs. "Only in your wildest dreams."

"See you're wearing your work purse. You just get off?"

"It's a briefcase." He side-eyes me. "And yes."

"Kinda late, no? You're not fucking around on River, are you?"

He barks out a laugh. "Please. Like I could find anyone better than her." His words are so sweet they almost make me queasy. "Post-season football shit."

"Sorry you guys sucked ass this year. But just so you know, that's entirely your fault, *Coach*."

"Fuck you very much," he mutters. "You hear from Maya about the rooms yet?"

I stiffen at the mention of her.

The crew wouldn't shut up about her for the first thirty minutes of lunch, grilling me about how I knew her and if I was "tapping that shit."

Jake finally steered the conversation in another direction after I snapped at the new kid when he mentioned how great Maya's ass looked in her jeans.

I mean, shit. He wasn't wrong, but he didn't need to bring

it up in conjunction with the half-chub he got from staring at it.

I shake my head. "Not yet."

"She'll come around."

I grunt.

Given my reaction to seeing her today, I'm not sure I *want* her to come around.

He turns to me. "What's that look for?"

"Nothing."

"Right. Like that same nothing that was happening at the bar?"

"Yep. Just like that."

He scoffs, settling back against the wall. "Gonna take a stab and guess you two met before we got there, and I bet you flirted your ass off because it's who you are. Then I'm going to guess you realized who she is and how off limits she is to you, huh?"

Fuck.

I kind of hate how well he knows me sometimes.

But I'm not going to give him the satisfaction of knowing whether he's right or wrong.

When I don't react, a slow, smug smile forms. "That's what I thought. Which makes this situation even better because you won't be trying to fuck her."

I ignore that part. "Thanks for that, by the way—putting us both on the spot, making me feel cornered into offering her a place."

He snorts. "Please. I've known you nearly all my life, Nolan. If I hadn't brought it up, you would have by the end of the night."

"Oh, I would have, huh?"

"Yep. Because as much as you try to act like a big grump who's all cold and closed off, not willing to do attachments, you're a secret softy."

I tip my chin up, rising to my full height. "Am not."

He laughs. "Right."

"I might be tired, but I'm not too tired to kick your ass."

He pushes off the wall as the elevator moves closer to his floor.

He doesn't seem the least bit afraid.

Really, he doesn't have a reason to.

We've been in a few scraps together over the years. Never anything major, just dumb shit, nothing a good punch or two couldn't fix. He might look like a goody-goody buttoned-up teacher during the day, but he can definitely hold his own.

"Go ahead and hit me, man. But just know you'll be the one having to explain to River why I came home with a black eye. She's the one you need to be afraid of."

He's not lying there.

The elevator dings, signaling it's reached his floor.

"Wanna come down for dinner?" he asks as the doors slide open. "We're doing pizza."

Pizza sounds a hell of a lot better than having the sandwich I skipped at lunch.

"Let me grab a shower first?"

"Please fucking do." He steps out and into the hall. "See you in a bit, soft serve."

I swear I hear him chuckle as the doors close.

Chapter 5

MAYA

"Are you shitting me?"

I glare down at my phone, my heart plummeting to the floor.

"What? What's wrong?" River asks, peering up from the box of Caroline's latest masterpieces as they go through them, sorting them out by collection.

It's crazy to see how far Caroline has come with her designs in the last few months alone. She started here as a sales associate back when I was married and volunteering my time to River to get out of the house. As soon as River and I discovered she had a hidden talent of creating super cute, one-of-a-kind designs, we knew we had to persuade her to let us sell them. We finally wore her down after the success of our pop-up at the Harristown Jubilee late last year.

"I got rejected."

"Again?"

"Damn." Caroline whistles. "This has to be some kind of record or something."

It sure feels like it.

In fact, it feels like the universe is doing everything in its power to ensure I become homeless.

"It doesn't help that everyone from Danford is looking for a place to stay too," Caroline points out, pulling another piece from the box and sorting it into its appropriate pile.

"I know we're mad at him right now, but can I just say how clever of a name that is? Dan Ford running *Danford* Apartments?" River slaps her leg, laughing. "Genius."

"I wish I could write 'struggling single mom' on the applications. Maybe it would gain me some sympathy points."

"Hate to say it, but it might actually hurt your chances."

Caroline may have a point there.

I hate the looks I get when people find out I'm a single mother to a twelve-year-old. It's either pity or judgment, especially when they find out how old I am and they do the math.

I bet several of the places I applied at passed on me based on my age and marital status alone, which is wrong on so many levels.

"Which apartments is it?"

I don't even know. I've applied to so many.

"It's the ones over on Hutton Street," I tell her, scanning the email for details. "It was a beautiful two-bedroom, two-bathroom place. Honestly, it's probably for the best. It was on the line of the school district and I probably would have had to fight with the administration about it." I groan, dropping my head to the counter, knocking it against the glass a few times. "I hope you weren't kidding about making Dean sleep on the couch, River, because at this rate, I'm never going to find a place, and I have less than two weeks left before I have to be out."

"I wasn't kidding, but I know of a better suggestion," River says, and I can guess where this is going. "You could say yes to Nolan."

I sigh.

"What?" She lifts her shoulders. "It'll fix all your problems."

Except the one where I can't stop thinking about him...

We're closing in on a week since Nolan made the offer for me to rent out his two rooms, and I still can't bring myself to accept it.

I keep holding out, hoping something will come through, but I'm beginning to worry nothing ever will.

When I bumped into him at The Gravy Train, I was surprised.

Never met the guy once before, and now I'm running into him everywhere.

Even without the dim lighting of the bar, Nolan's handsome.

In truth, the reaction I have to him is part of the reason I'm hesitant to say yes.

Sure, he's off limits to my brain. But to my neglected lady bits? Well, they aren't getting the memo, especially not when he pierces me with that blue stare of his.

"I'm with River on this one," Caroline says. "If you're worrying about living with a hot guy, don't. It's not that bad. I lived with Cooper for years without a problem."

River twists her lips up. "I'm not sure you're allowed to use that as an example considering you're now screwing each other's brains out."

"We're not *screwing each other's brains out*. It's called *love*."

59

"Uh-huh. Love and wild passionate sex where you let him do some *very* naughty things to you."

"River!" Caroline admonishes. "I told you all that in confidence!"

"Um, excuse me," I interrupt. "Why haven't I heard about these naughty things?"

They exchange a glance, and understanding dawns.

"Oh," I say. "Because I'm single, right?"

They have the gall to appear sheepish.

"We didn't want to make you…"

"Jealous."

Caroline shakes her head, her blonde hair bouncing with the movement. "No—sad."

"Guys, I'm divorced, not dead. We can still talk about sex and stuff."

"Yeah, but you're not getting any."

"And it's been forever since you've even gone out," River adds. "You should try to get back out there."

It's not that I don't want to get back out there. Hell, I'd *love* to get back in the dating game and get some action, but it's harder than they think.

Finding someone to date is difficult already. Add a kid to the mix and it gets about ten times harder. Most people our age don't want that sort of commitment so soon.

And I get it. I do.

I just hope I don't spend the next ten years searching for a guy who's interested in me, my kid, and all the baggage that comes with co-parenting. I can't imagine being alone for so long.

But my lack of love life isn't what's important right now.

"I think I should be focusing on where I'm going to live rather than the sad state of my sex life."

"Again, might I suggest Nolan?" River says.

"To help with my sex life or my living situation?"

"Why not both?"

River and I exchange a look, then burst out laughing.

"I was teasing, Caroline, you little oversexed hussy."

Her cheeks pinken. "It's Cooper's fault."

My chest constricts, the pang of envy hitting me again.

"Besides, if—and that's a big if—I'm going to say yes to Nolan's offer, there will be *no* sleeping together."

"It's only temporary. Why not have a little fun in the meantime?"

"Hey, hi." River raises her hand. "I tried that once. Didn't work."

"Yeah, but you and Dean were circling each other way before he moved into your place. That's different."

Caroline makes a fair point. River and Dean spent the better part of a year claiming they hated each other—all because Dean was *allegedly* an ass about River's cat when he first moved in—before being forced into close quarters together finally made them face their feelings.

"This is a pointless conversation because I won't be sleeping with him. I'm not sure when I even indicated I was interested in him."

"You have eyes," Caroline says. "Don't pretend that man isn't hot."

"Where have *you* seen him?" I ask.

"I know what the internet is."

River laughs. "Caroline's right. Nolan is hot, but Maya has the right approach for when she does accept the offer."

"Really?" Caroline says, twisting her lips up. "I thought since it worked out so well for you, you'd be all for it."

"Well, Nolan's not the commitment type. Dean says he's never had a relationship last longer than a few weeks. I highly doubt Maya wants to get into something like that when she has Sam to worry about too."

I point to River. "Exactly."

"You can always sneak around," Caroline suggests. "Sam would never have to know."

"My god," River mutters. "What happened to our sweet, innocent Caroline?" Another blush steals up her cheeks, and River rolls her eyes. "Never mind. *Cooper.*"

She says his name mockingly, and I laugh because River is the same way over Dean, even if she doesn't want to admit it half the time.

"Again, moot point. Not sleeping with him. I barely know him."

Not that it was going to stop me before…

River slides her eyes my way, and something flashes in her gaze that I'm having a hard time deciphering, which hasn't happened in a long time.

It's gone as quickly as it came, and I wonder if I imagined it.

"But you are saying yes to him, right?" she questions.

I sigh. "I'll think about it."

"Well, you better think hard. We're down to the wire here."

Like I need the reminder.

The clock is ticking away. It's all I hear when I close my eyes at night.

"I know," I tell her. "I have one other application out. If I don't hear anything by Friday, I'll accept."

It's a lie, but she doesn't need to know that.

She seems pleased enough by my answer, a tight-lipped smile pulling at her face. "Okay. Now, let's get to work. We have about three more boxes to get through before we can close. I want to get home at a decent hour tonight. Dean's making me chicken Alfredo, and I can't wait to make fun of him when he inevitably messes it up."

Me: Can we talk?

With a heavy sigh, I set my phone down next to the stove, then return my attention to the task at hand: spaghetti.

After my major letdown of being rejected again yesterday, I finally stumbled upon some good news.

A new build I applied to previously is extending their leasing…in two months. It's within the school zone limits *and* my price range. Assuming my credit and background checks come back good—which I know they will—we're unofficially in.

This means, if everything goes as planned, I'll only have to put my pride aside and accept Nolan's offer for two months.

I check my phone to see if he's texted back yet.

Nothing.

Dammit.

"Hey, Mom?"

"Hmm?" I say, not looking up from the red sauce I've

been stirring the past few minutes. I shake more salt into the mixture, then give it a taste.

Almost there. Needs a bit more salt.

Aside from all the great memories I created with Sam, being a stay-at-home mom gave me something else I'm grateful for—the ability to cook a decent meal.

I'm not a chef by any stretch of the imagination, but I know my way around the kitchen well enough. I spent a lot of time in one when Sam was a baby, always trying new recipes I could impress my husband with.

That was back when I thought Patrick and I could make something of our future.

That feeling didn't last long.

"Should I start packing up my room?"

I drop the spoon into the pot of sauce, and red liquid goes flying onto the stovetop.

"Shit," I mutter, retrieving the messy spoon and tapping it against the rim of the pot to clean it off. I cup my hand to catch any drips and spin toward the sink. I switch the water on, rinsing it off, and peek over at Sam. His head is bent as he works on his math homework. "What do you mean?"

"They're starting construction soon, aren't they?"

"How do you know that?"

He lifts his shoulders. "Katlyn told me."

"Mr. Dan's daughter?"

"Yeah. We play Minecraft together. She has leukemia, so she's on there a lot because she doesn't have to go to school anymore."

I didn't ask Dan what Katlyn's illness was, but part of me figured it was cancer. It would explain his desperation for financial help. Chemo isn't cheap.

"Should I pack up my room before I go to Dad's? Will I have to pack up my PlayStation? Can I still go to the game?"

I sigh.

I haven't talked to Sam about the move much since I got the first letter. I told him we'd be moving soon because of the sale, but I haven't brought it up since.

A mistake on my part. It's his life getting uprooted too, and I should have been more considerate of that. I just didn't want to burden him with the semantics of everything that comes along with moving. The kid is already aware of how much I struggle to make sure he's able to take part in other things kids with two active parents can. I didn't need him to worry about this too.

I shut off the water, setting the spoon back next to the stove, then switch the sauce down to a simmer and cover the pot.

I twist back around to Sam, leaning against the counter until we're eye level.

"I wanted to talk to you about that…"

He peeks up from his homework. "About the hockey game? I can't go?"

"No, it's not about that. You can still go." He relaxes. "It's about where we'll be living."

"Are we staying with Aunt River and Dean?"

I frown. "No, but we'll be staying in the same building. You remember Dean's friend Nolan? The one you played football with?"

He bobs his head up and down. "Yep. I remember Dean hit him in the nuts with the football and he cried."

Hearing my kid refer to his balls as nuts is not something I was expecting, but I breeze past it. "Well, he recently moved in and happens to need a few roommates."

"Okay." He nods, absorbing the news. "Why do we have to stay there?"

"Because we're on the waiting list for an apartment, but it's not available for another two months."

He twists his lips up, considering it. "Will I have my own room like now?"

I nod. "Yep."

That is what Nolan said, right? Man, I wish he'd text me back already.

"Does Nolan play video games?"

"I'm not sure."

"Can you find out?"

I chuckle, because of course he's most concerned about if Nolan plays video games. He's twelve.

"Yeah, I can find out."

"Cool."

"So, you're good with it?"

He shrugs again. "Yep."

"Cool," I repeat back to him. "Now put your homework aside and set the table. Dinner is about ready."

By some miracle, he doesn't argue and hops down from the stool at the bar.

My phone buzzes against the counter, and I race to grab it.

I can't help the grin on my face when I see his name on my phone.

I saved his number under Romeo in a spur-of-the-moment decision.

Romeo: What's up?

Me: Are those rooms still available?

Romeo: Can we talk on the phone? I hate texting.

My heart rate skyrockets.

Fuck. Did he find a roommate already? Did I blow my chances by dragging my feet?

Romeo: I should have led with, "Yes, they're still available."

I breathe a sigh of relief.

Me: Call you around 9? Sitting down to eat.

Romeo: K

A surge of irritation runs through me.

K?

He knows that's the texting equivalent of *Go fuck yourself*, right?

Romeo: I probably should have said "Okay" or "Sounds good."

Romeo: Dean always yells at me for just typing K.

Romeo: Told you I'm bad at texting.

I giggle, liking the way he keeps using quotations. It's cute.

Me: It's fine. Talk to you soon.

Sam sets the table as I plate the spaghetti, then I pull the garlic bread from the oven and slip it into a napkin and basket like they do at the restaurants because it makes Sam smile.

We chat about his school day over dinner, and afterward, he loads up the dishwasher while I handwash the pots and pans.

"Can I go play Minecraft?" he asks when he's finished.

"Is your homework done?"

"Yes. I have two questions left but I don't understand them, so I'm going to ask Mr. Evans for help in the morning."

"It's math homework, right?" He nods. "Why are you asking Dean to help with math? He teaches English."

He shrugs. "Everyone goes to Mr. Evans with homework help. He's, like, the coolest teacher we have."

A smile pulls at my lips. River snagged herself a good one.

"Then yes, you can play—after you shower. You're starting to smell like a teenage boy, and you're not even a teenager yet."

"Next month!" he singsongs over his shoulder as he meanders down the hall to the bathroom.

A knot forms in my stomach at the reminder.

Where has the time gone? Has it been thirteen years since my world was flipped upside down?

Sometimes it feels like just yesterday I was sitting in River's bathroom, four positive pregnancy tests sitting on the counter as she wrapped her arms around me and held me as I cried.

I pull myself from the past and finish cleaning up the kitchen. I move into the living room next, where I find at least two pairs of socks under the couch that certainly don't belong to me, and then I fold a load of laundry and set the fresh clothes on Sam's bed.

It's eight by the time I make my way to my bedroom to finally get out of my work clothes.

I chuckle as I pass the bathroom, hearing Sam in there singing a song at least thirty years older than he is.

He really needs to stop hanging out with Dean so much.

After trading my jeans for a pair of jogger sweats and my flowery blouse for an old t-shirt with one too many holes in it, I see I still have almost another hour until I have to call Nolan. I try to pass the time by making a list of everything I'll need to do to get ready for the move, but every time I glance at the clock, only a minute or two has passed.

When eight forty-five finally rolls around, I make Sam shut off his game and brush his teeth.

By nine, he's in bed, and I'm pouring a glass of wine to calm my racing mind.

I climb into my queen-sized bed and fire up the TV I hardly use to distract myself. There's some reality show playing, and I allow myself to zone out for a few minutes while I gather courage.

I don't know why my heart is racing. I've never been too shy to pick up the phone and talk to someone. But for some reason, calling Nolan is sending my nerves into overdrive.

You're being ridiculous, Maya. Just call the man and accept his offer. It's not that hard.

I tip my wine back again, then with a deep breath, I pull up his number on my phone and hit the call icon before I can talk myself out of it.

It rings once before I even bring the phone to my ear.

Then again.

A third time.

And then a fourth.

I'm about to hang up when I hear a groggy voice on the other end of the line.

"'Lo?"

My brows pull together and I glance at the phone to make sure I called the right number. "Nolan?"

"Yeah." He clears his throat. "Maya?"

"Were you, uh, sleeping?"

"Shit," he mutters, then he sighs, and I hear rustling. "Sorry. Yeah. I guess I was."

"Is this a bad time?"

"No." Another sigh. "I was just up early this morning and had a long day."

"Oh. Do you work early often?"

"I do four tens a week, so yes."

"Oh."

Why do I keep saying oh?

I hear him moving around and what sounds like a cup being pulled from the cupboard. Ice clinks against a glass, then there's the telltale hiss of water moving through pipes. He gulps a few times, then smacks his lips together.

"I take it you weren't able to find anything else?"

"No." This time it's me who clears their throat. "Well, technically yes, but the apartments aren't available for another two months, so in the meantime…"

"You're wanting to rent my rooms."

I nod, which is dumb because he can't see me. "Yes. Is that okay?"

I picture him leaning against the counter in his kitchen, folding his big arms over his chest. "I wouldn't have offered if it wasn't."

"Right." I take a sip of my wine. "It's kind of short notice, but we'd need to move in rather quickly."

"That's fine."

"Are you sure?"

He sighs again, and I don't know him well enough to know if it's an irritated sound or not. "Yes. Are you free tomorrow?"

"You want me to move in *tomorrow*?"

It comes out as a squeal.

He chuckles, the deep sound rumbling through my phone. "No. Well, I mean if you need to, then yes. It just so happens I'm off work tomorrow since I put in a shift over the weekend. You could come by and check out the apartment if you want. You know, to make sure my ax is locked up tight and no other murder weapons are lying around."

His teasing makes me laugh, and for the first time since I texted him, I relax.

"I'd appreciate that. I don't go in until noon, so tomorrow is fine."

"Want to meet for breakfast at The Gravy Train and then walk over afterward?"

"That sounds good."

"Okay."

The line goes quiet, and I check the phone to see if he's still there.

He is.

We just don't know how to end this call.

"So, uh, what are you wearing?"

I almost spit my wine out. "What?!"

He laughs. "I'm kidding. Just thought I'd break the tension."

"Living with you is going to be fun."

He mutters something I can't quite make out.

And a thought hits me.

"How much?"

"Huh?"

"The rent—how much is the rent?"

"Six fifty."

What? There's no way… "That seems way too good to be true."

"Well, it's true."

"You're not trying to cut me some pity deal, are you?"

"I don't know you very well just yet, Maya, but I have a feeling you wouldn't appreciate me saying yes to that."

"You're damn right I wouldn't."

"Then no, that's not what I'm doing."

"Nolan…" I sigh, closing my eyes against the tears forming. Part of me wants to argue with him. The other part is grateful. "Thank you."

He doesn't say anything, and I'm glad he doesn't say anything.

I've been an emotional wreck for weeks now. If he were to say something, the dam barely keeping my tears at bay would certainly burst.

"So, does nine tomorrow work?" he asks.

It gives me enough time to get Sam to school and get back across town. "Yes, nine is fine."

"Sounds good."

"Uh…" I'm at a loss for how to end the conversation. "Good night then."

He chuckles lightly, like he knows how uncomfortable I am. "Night, Juliet."

A smile breaks out across my face as the call disconnects.

That night, for the first time in a long while, I sleep peacefully.

Chapter 6

NOLAN

Maya: I'm running five minutes late. I'm sorry.

Me: I hope this isn't an indication of how you pay the rent…

Maya: I'll have you know I'm an excellent tenant.

Me: This isn't helping your case at all.

Maya: Blame the school drop-off line, not me.

Me: Uh-huh. Likely excuse.

Maya: Shut up.

Maya: OMW

Me: OMW?

Me: Never mind. Google helped me.

I tuck my phone into my pocket, then run a hand through my still wet hair as I lean against the back wall of the elevator.

At the rate this thing moves, I'll be running five minutes late too.

As I watch the floors tick by at a snail's pace, I do a mental check of the apartment.

Fuck. I should have done one last sweep, made sure

everything is in decent shape since I'll be bringing Maya back there.

I laugh to myself as the elevator finally stops in the lobby.

Man, if you'd have told me when I met her I'd be bringing her back to my place, I'd have thought it was because I was about to get my dick wet, not for her to inspect it before she moves in.

The thought literally stops me in my tracks, right in the doorway of the apartment building.

"Thanks," someone chirps as they slide past me, thinking I'm holding the door open for them.

I'm not.

I'm too fucking busy freaking out.

I give myself a shake, shove my hands in my pockets, and keep walking.

I almost bump into a pole, then a person, so lost in my thoughts as I make the short walk to the diner.

What the fuck am I thinking?

She can't live with me. Her kid sure as fuck can't live with me either.

I can't afford to get attached, not even in the slightest—and Maya is the type of person you could get attached to.

I need to tell her this is off.

I can't do this.

I—

"Hey!"

Her voice hits my ears, and my eyes snap to her as she sashays down the sidewalk toward me.

She's wearing a smile that takes up her whole face, and her gray eyes are brighter than I've seen them yet. She somehow looks years younger, and I know it's the stress leaving her body that does it.

Seeing how much of a difference this is making for her when she hasn't even moved in yet...I'd be an asshole to say no.

"Hey," I say as she comes to a stop in front of me. "Glad you could finally make it."

Her eyes narrow to slits, only there's nothing but humor in them. "Says the guy also running late."

"Blame the slow-as-shit elevator, not me."

"Uh-huh. Likely excuse," she quips, feeding my words back to me.

I grin, then nod toward the diner. "You ready?"

"Please. I am starving this morning. I've been so stressed these last few weeks I've not been eating much. I guess it's finally catching up with me."

"Let's get you fed then."

I pull the door open and place my hand on the small of her back, guiding her in.

We place our order with Darlene, who is surprised to see us together, then we grab a booth toward the back.

"You seem friendly with Darlene. Do you come here often?" Maya asks.

She strips off her jacket, then tosses it onto the bench beside her. She's wearing another cute-as-hell beanie and pulls it off too. She runs a hand through her long hair, brushing it out over her shoulder, then sets her chin in her hand, locking her gaze onto mine.

I wonder if I'll ever get used to how startling her eyes are.

I try to ignore how uncomfortable her stare is making me.

Not because I don't like being the subject of her attention, but because it's like she's looking *at* me…*into* me.

I nod. "Especially now that I live up the block. Before, when I lived on the outskirts of town, I tried to make the trip once a week or so. You?"

"Almost every Sunday to have breakfast with River, and I usually do a coffee run or two during the week."

"Well, full disclosure, I'll likely be bringing it home a couple nights a week. I'm not the best cook."

She lifts a shoulder. "Fine by me, but I should note I know my way around the kitchen fairly well. If you're interested in me making dinner, that is."

I want to tell her she doesn't have to cook me dinner, that all she needs to do is pay the rent and we're good.

But I have a feeling she'll argue with me.

"I'll keep that in mind," I say instead.

"Here's your coffee, dear." My favorite server, Darlene, slides a cup of black coffee in front of me. "And yours, Ms. Maya." She sets another cup in front of Maya alongside a small plate with little packets on it. "Plus your sugar and cream."

Maya beams up at her. "Thanks, Dar. I forgot to add, can you make sure they don't—"

"Put any powdered sugar on your French toast? I got you, babe."

She gives us a wink, then slinks away.

Maya plucks a single thing of creamer and two packets of sugar from the plate. She dumps them into her coffee, then dunks her spoon into the steaming liquid and stirs.

She lifts the hot cup to her lips, blowing on it.

"What?" she asks when she realizes I'm staring at her.

"What kind of criminal passes on powdered sugar on their French toast? That's half the reason you order French toast. The other half is the syrup."

"Then I'm really about to blow your mind when I don't use any." She laughs when my jaw drops. "Unless it's fruit, I'm not a big sweets person."

"But I just watched you put two packets of sugar in your coffee."

"One and a half. It's about all I can handle too."

"So no sweets at all?"

She takes a sip of her coffee. "I didn't say that."

"You're just selective about your sweets," I guess.

"Yes."

"Cake?"

She shrugs. "Nah."

"Ice cream?"

"If I'm in the mood."

"Brownies?"

"Eh. Not a fan, especially if they have nuts in them."

"Obviously. That's sacrilege."

She grins. "I see we'll get along just fine."

"So, no cake, ice cream, or brownies." I run a hand over my freshly shaved face. "What *do* you like, then?"

"You really want to know?"

"Yes."

She leans across the table like she's getting ready to tell me all the lost secrets of the world. "It's kind of specific."

I match her movement, eager to hear what she has to say.

"Hit me with it."

"Christmas Trees."

"Christmas trees?"

She nods. "Yep. Those Little Debbie cakes that come out around Christmastime."

"Aren't those the same as Zebra Cakes?"

She gasps. "Blasphemous! You bite your tongue!"

"But—"

"No." She holds her hand up. "Don't you dare try to defile the legacy of my trees by equating them to *Zebra Cakes.*"

She curls her lips as she says *Zebra Cakes*, and I do my best not to laugh.

This is clearly a hot-button issue for her.

"My apologies," I say, taking a swallow of my coffee so she can't see my smile. "Do you stockpile them so you can have them throughout the year?"

"No way. That's half the magic of them—that they're only available once a year. They tried to do a 'Christmas in July' edition once, and they didn't taste the same. I made sure to send a feedback email too."

"I'm sure they took your comments straight up the ladder."

"I hope so."

I tuck my lips together, shaking my head. "You're something else."

Her face falls. "Oh god. You think I'm insane, don't you? I promise I'm not. I'm just a little in love with my Christmas Trees is all. I'm perfectly stable the other nine months of the year."

"Not insane...*passionate.*"

She captures her bottom lip between her teeth, and my blood flows to areas it shouldn't.

"That's a good thing, right?" she asks, blinking up at me with those tantalizing eyes.

It's the same look she gave me in the bar.

Impish and sexy.

Inviting.

I want to reach over the table, pull her into my lap, and finally get a taste of her lips.

Fuck. I can't be thinking like this.

If Maya is going to be staying at my place for two months, I can't be conjuring up images of kissing her or anything else my brain has cooked up over the last week...like that fantasy of—

No! Nope.

Not going there.

"Sure." I swallow, working hard to talk my dick down. I clear my throat and cast my eyes anywhere but her. "So, I guess we should talk about the details of your lease."

"Right." She retreats to her side, pressing her shoulders back. "Like I said last night, it'll only be for two months while they finish up the new apartments over off Burrow Street."

"I know the ones. That land was bought by a rival company. I didn't realize they were leasing already."

"They had opened up a few rentals around when we got the notice of the demolition, but they filled up fast. I guess they're ready to move on to phase two soon."

"Lucky for you then."

"I'd be even luckier if I didn't have to do this at all." She waves her hand. "Whatever. It's all finally working out."

I see it again, that relief in her gaze.

Darlene brings breakfast out: French toast sans syrup and powdered sugar for Maya and a stack of syrup and whipped-cream-covered pancakes with a side of bacon *and* sausage for me.

We tuck into our food, taking a break from talking to get some fuel in our stomachs.

"You can charge me more, you know," Maya says after a few minutes of silence. "I'm good for it."

"I don't doubt that, but I can't in good conscience charge you more when you're only staying for two months. Especially not when you're going to have to put down a deposit and everything else that comes with a new apartment so soon."

"But your savings..."

"Will be fine," I tell her.

She doesn't need to know the money I have in there hasn't been touched to cover the extra expenses the apartment upgrade cost me. I make enough to cover the rent without digging into it and can still get by.

In truth, I was in no real hurry to get a roommate, which is why I've been dragging my feet about it the last few months. I'm enjoying having such a big space to myself for the first time.

Besides, I haven't done anything except work for the last ten years. I don't go out often, and I don't spend money on frivolous things. Even with the added expense, my savings account is doing fine.

"If you're sure..."

I don't bother dignifying that with a response.

"Right." She wipes a napkin across her lips, then tosses it next to her plate.

"Are you not going to finish that?" I ask, nodding toward the leftover French toast.

"Just taking a break." She sinks farther into the booth, expelling a heavy breath, and points a finger my way. "Don't even think about reaching over here and stealing it. I will stab you."

"That's the second death threat I've received from you. And you were worried I'd be the murderer."

"I'm still not convinced you're not. But speaking of our arrangement...I promised Sam his own room. I wasn't wrong to do that, right?"

"He'll have his own room."

Now that I'm thinking about it, maybe Maya should be the one to bunk in my library. I'd rather not have the kid's grubby hands all over my collection.

"How old is Sam?"

"He'll be thirteen at the end of next month."

Her eyes light up again, this time for a different reason.

This time it's with pure love and devotion.

"If you're wondering if he's a little shit, the answer is yes, sometimes. He likes to roll his eyes and whine and sometimes talk back, but in general, he's a good kid. Quiet, keeps to himself mostly, and, barring the stray pair or two of socks, picks up after himself."

I chuckle. "That's good to know. I'll make sure to watch out for the socks though."

She tilts her head, studying me. "You're not a kid person, are you?"

I can lie.

I can tell her I love the little fucks.

But I have a feeling she'd see right through me.

"I'm not *against* them, but I'm not actively trying to have them either."

She laughs. "I appreciate the honesty. I wasn't either at first. I felt so awful because I didn't like Sam when he was first born. I mean, I *loved* him, but I didn't *like* him, you know?" She smiles fondly at the memory. "Then, one day when he was particularly fussy, screaming and crying like mad, I lost my cool and screamed right back. He stopped, lifted his little barely there brows, then giggled. Something clicked for me when I heard that sound."

Over the years, when I've expressed my disinterest in kids, I've always gotten the response of *Just wait* or *It's different when they're yours*, like I'm magically going to change my mind.

I like how Maya is honest about how her connection with her son wasn't instantaneous.

I like how real she is.

"So, you're against love and kids. What else are you against?"

"Onions."

"Onions?"

"Yep." I nod. "Fucking disgusting if you ask me."

"Extra onions on your meals—got it."

I lean across the table. "I will look you dead in the eye and scrape the food you worked so hard on right into the trash and feel nothing as I do it."

She blinks twice, then tosses her head back and laughs.

It's loud, drawing the attention of others, I'm sure.

But neither of us give a shit.

I can't take my eyes off her.

Maya is gorgeous in this moment, and I'm enraptured by her.

After several seconds, she gathers herself, wiping at her eyes with her fingertips.

"I think our arrangement is going to work out just fine, Romeo."

"Yeah?"

A slow smile pulls at her lips, and there's a twinkle in her eye. "Yeah."

"So, this is it," I say as I push open the door to my apartment.

She slips past me and into my new haven.

I stand in the entryway as she stalks around the living room, taking everything in.

There's not much, no art on the walls or anything that pops. Just a plain gray single recliner and a black coffee table that has seen better days. My TV rests on a console I found on the side of the road, and it's filled with odd-and-end knickknacks and a couple of box sets of TV shows I love.

The floor plan is open, and since I don't yet have a kitchen table and eat at the counter, the space appears extra empty.

"It's cute," she says, glancing at me over her shoulder.

"It's shit and we both know it."

"Well, now that you mention it…"

I chuckle. "I'm not much of a decorator."

Plus, I don't spend a lot of time out here. I'd rather hang in my bedroom, where my big TV is, or my library.

"Not everyone has *the touch*. I can help if you'd like."

My first instinct is to say no. I don't need her coming in here messing up my space when she'll only be around for two months.

But she looks so excited to help, so I find myself nodding.

She flashes me a bright smile, and there's a strange pull in my chest at the sight.

She points to the hallway. "Rooms?"

I nod and finally move from my spot, making my way down the hall. She follows behind me, so close I can feel her body heat coming off her.

I stop at the first room and push the door open. "This one is empty."

Her brows pull together. "Is the other one not?"

I shake my head and walk to the next room that's directly across the hall from mine, opening the door.

She steps into the space, her jaw dropping.

"Wow." The word comes out a whisper. "I was not expecting this."

I lean against the doorframe, crossing my arms over my chest as she takes in the eight shelves lining the back wall, each full of books.

I've wanted my own library for years, and having this space is a big reason I said yes to this apartment, even though it was bigger than I had planned to go.

The first thing I did when I moved in was set up this room. I built my bookshelves and got my books out of those awful boxes they'd been in for far too many years, then took my time finding the perfect reading chair and lamp to complete the space.

It's not much, but it's mine.

"What? Big, dumb welder can't read?"

She side-eyes me. "I didn't say that. I'm...surprised you have so many books."

I shrug. "It's not that many."

"It's eight full shelves. That's a lot more than most people."

I push off the frame, stalking into the room. I crouch in front of the shelf farthest away, the one that has some space when I move a few books around. "They aren't full...yet."

"So, you're a big reader, huh?"

"Yep."

"Have you always been?"

"No." I push to my full height again. "I used to be absolute shit in school and could barely read for a long time. It wasn't until Dean caught on to my lack of reading comprehension skills and named himself my official tutor that I got better at it. I'm still not the best reader, but it doesn't hold me back like it used to."

What I don't tell her is I used to love it when my mom read to me, and it was my favorite thing in the world...until she left.

After, I didn't give a shit about reading anymore, and it's the reason I fell so far behind.

She stares up at me, and the surprise in her eyes is evident.

I'm not embarrassed by the fact that I struggled with reading, but it's not something I talk about often either.

"What's your favorite book?"

"It's kind of a silly one." I walk over to the shelf that has my favorites and pluck the book from among the others. *The Lion, the Witch and the Wardrobe* by C.S. Lewis. Sure, it's a little juvenile, but it's the first book I finished in one sitting."

She takes the book from my hands, running her perfectly manicured fingers over the tattered front cover. There's a smile tugging at her kissable lips.

"It's not juvenile. It's…sweet." She giggles. "Which is kind of a funny word for you."

"Because of the big, dumb welder thing?"

She rolls her eyes, then slips the book back into its spot.

Her hand lands on my chest, patting it twice, and I swear I feel her touch down to my fucking toes. "We'll go with that."

I glance down at where her hand rests on my chest, and her eyes follow the movement.

Like she's only now realized she's touching me, she withdraws her hand like she's been holding it on top of a hot stove and takes my breath right with it.

If she heard, she gives no indication.

What kind of idiot gets riled up over a pat?

For fuck's sake, I need to get laid or something.

Or get a damn grip.

I swallow, giving myself a mental shake, and clear my throat.

"I was thinking this could be your room," I tell her. "I can move the chair to my bedroom so there's enough room for a bed and whatever else you'll need."

"Because you don't trust my kid in here around your books?"

I cringe when she says it aloud, and she barks out a laugh when my face crumples, caught.

"It's fine. I understand. I wouldn't trust him either. Like I said, he can be a shit sometimes."

Relief floods me. "I'm glad we're on the same page."

"So, three bedrooms—I assume that means two bathrooms?"

I nod, then point down the hallway. "End of the hall.

Though I don't ever use it for some reason, so I'll have to hit the store to grab some supplies for in there."

"You don't need to do that," she says. "I can get everything."

I nod but have no intentions of letting that happen.

"You mentioned it would need to be a quick move-in. Did you have a date in mind?"

"Is Monday too soon? If so, I can figure something out. I have Thursdays off too. I need to vacate my apartment by the end of the month—though I suspect you already knew that."

"Hey, I just show up on the jobsite and go where I'm told. That's it."

She laughs. "I'm teasing. But you have to admit this whole situation is rather comical. I mean, what are the odds?"

I think back to that first night in the bar.

I was going to bring her home with me. We know where the night was leading. We were ready for it.

Then everything blew up.

"It's an…interesting situation, that's for sure."

She tucks her hands into her back pockets, then rocks back on her heels. "So…are we going to talk about it?"

"Talk about what?" I ask, playing dumb.

"The fact that I was going to go home with you that Friday night. I'm going to be living with you, so we should probably discuss it at some point."

I hoped we'd pretend it never happened, but…

"But you didn't. There's nothing to discuss. No harm, no foul. Just a…missed connection."

She tilts her head again, and I've learned she does that when she's trying to figure me out.

She stares at me so long I start to feel uncomfortable under her gaze.

Or maybe I don't want her to see right through me.

Finally, she sighs, nodding once. "Okay. It never happened then. So, move-in day?"

Chapter 7

MAYA

I didn't stay much longer at Nolan's, the mood shifting firmly into awkwardness.

We settled on Monday, the day the boutique is closed, and a day Nolan happened to have off.

It didn't leave me much time to get things packed, but I managed to tape up the last box minutes before Nolan arrived.

He's prompt, I'll give him that.

But I appreciate it since I'm dead tired and already looking forward to getting this day over with so I can crawl into bed and rest. I have never been more thankful for Patrick's shitty work schedule in my life. We switched weeks around and it worked out perfectly that Sam's at his father's during this whole mess of moving.

"Is this everything?" He peers around the bare apartment. "It's not much."

He's right. It's not.

When I moved out of Patrick's, I was starting over. I didn't want to be burdened by things of my past, so I packed light.

I would have thought in the last two years I'd fill in the missing spaces, but I haven't.

That's definitely a blessing right now.

"I figured we could move my couch in while we're staying there if you're okay with that. Other than that, the only other big stuff is our beds and Sam's desk. I put everything else in storage. Hopefully, we won't be there long, so no need to move all the large items several times."

"Did you hire someone to move your furniture? Because I have a truck…"

"It's no big deal." I wave my hand. "I had some people who are still left in the building help out. There are a few older guys downstairs I paid in beer and pizza, so whatever."

And a hundred bucks, but he doesn't need to know that.

He nods. "All right. Let's get this all loaded up then. Should take only two trips."

I help Nolan load his truck, and I'm grateful he doesn't try to pull the shit most guys do and make me sit on the sidelines because I'm a woman.

By the time we have the first load strapped in—which is mostly our beds and Sam's desk—I'm sweating.

"You good?" Nolan asks as I lean against the tailgate of his truck, working to catch my breath.

He takes up the spot next to me, folding those big arms of his over his chest, his green flannel shirt stretching across his muscles.

I don't even have the energy to focus on how close he's standing and how even though we've been moving stuff for the last hour and sweating, he still smells so damn good.

"Yeah. Just tired." As if on cue, my stomach growls.

Nolan chuckles. "And hungry apparently."

"Guilty. I didn't get a chance to eat this morning. Too busy worrying about getting everything packed, and I forgot."

"Want to grab something on the way to our place?"

Our place.

His phrasing sends a tingle down my spine.

I like that he does that—doesn't make me feel like I'm intruding on his space. To him, no matter how short my stay is, this is my apartment too. It helps lessen how much I feel like a burden.

"If it's not too much trouble…"

He shakes his head, pushing off the truck and moving around to the driver's side. "Not at all. I could use something myself. Had to get some blood work done this morning, so I should probably eat something."

I shift my head back. "Blood work? Is everything okay?"

"Yep. Just a checkup."

"You get checkups?"

He tilts his head, furrowing his brows, looking at me over the bed of the truck. "Aren't I supposed to?"

"Well, yeah. I guess I'm just surprised. Most guys don't do the doctor. You have to twist their arms to get them to go."

"Most guys or your ex?"

My cheeks heat. "Well, I guess he's really the only guy I've ever known in that capacity."

Something flashes in his eyes, but I'm not quite sure what it is. It's gone just as fast as he drops his gaze and gets into the truck.

I follow his lead, hopping into the other side.

He doesn't say anything again until we're pulling onto the road.

"My dad died of lung cancer five years ago. He owned a

body shop and spent a lot of time in a paint booth. Due to the nature of my job, I get my lungs checked once a year to be safe. I hadn't had my blood work done in a couple of years, so we went ahead and did that too."

My heart drops. "I'm sorry. I…I didn't realize."

He lifts his big shoulders. "It's okay. No harm, no foul."

It's the second time he's said that, and I hate it less this time than the first.

"Was he…sick for long?"

I don't know why I ask it, but I can't take it back.

"I'm not sure. He hid it for a long time, coughing up blood and stuff. He didn't think it was a big deal, I guess. He passed about a month after he was diagnosed."

My heart aches for him. I've never had to watch a loved one die, and I can't imagine what that must feel like.

"You remind me of him," he says, surprising me.

"I do?"

He nods. "He was a single parent, too. Stubborn as shit. Never wanting to ask anyone for help. Determined to make it by on his own."

"You calling me stubborn, Romeo?"

His lips twitch. "Maybe. But my dad, he was strong too. Resilient. I haven't known you long, but from what I've seen, you fit that bill exactly."

He slides his eyes my way, and my heart flutters at the honesty I see shining in them.

I blink back my tears, shifting in the passenger seat of the truck at the attention. "Thank you," I whisper.

"Welcome."

He pulls into a fast-food place and we grab a couple of

sausage biscuits and hash browns. He must be starving because he gets enough food for four people. I try to pay, but he ignores my efforts.

We're both so famished we don't talk the rest of the ride, too busy stuffing our faces on the way to the apartment.

Nolan parks the truck right in front of the building as I'm tossing the last hash brown into my mouth, then he pulls his phone from his pocket.

He presses a few buttons, then holds it up to his ear.

"Hey," he says when whoever he's calling answers. "Yep. Downstairs. Thanks, man."

He hangs up, then tosses his phone into the cup holder.

I raise my brows at him.

"I called Cooper."

"Like *Cooper* Cooper?"

"Yeah, we've been hanging out since I moved in here. He's gonna help us get this shit upstairs. No offense, but you are not built for moving bulky furniture."

I laugh. "No offense taken. Honestly, I was starting to hate myself a little for not planning this better and getting someone to help."

We hop out of the truck as Cooper ambles out of the building.

"Hey, Maya," Cooper says, giving me a quick hug. "Glad to finally have you in the building. Caroline won't shut up about all the girls' nights she, you, and River are going to have." He leans in conspiratorially. "Honestly, I can't wait to get her out of my hair. Her *Vampire Diaries* obsession has reached a new high, and I need a break from all the undead drama."

I roll my eyes, shoving his shoulder playfully. "Stop acting like you aren't addicted too."

He can act like he wants a break from Caroline all he wants, but he's so obviously smitten with her I know he's full of shit.

"Little help would be nice."

We snap our attention to Nolan at his harsh tone. He's practically scowling our way, his brows extra furrowed.

Okay then...

Cooper raises his brows at me before turning to Nolan with a smirk. "Sorry, man."

Nolan and Cooper spend the next hour unloading the truck —twice as quickly as we got it loaded—while I take a much-needed break.

Cooper stays behind to work while we head back to my place for the next load.

After a few mishaps with boxes that were poorly taped together—completely my fault—we're getting the last of the items into the apartment when dinnertime rolls around.

My feet hurt. My back is on fire. And I'm so damn hungry I'm starting to feel queasy.

I'm ready for food, a glass of wine, and a bed.

"You good with grabbing something for dinner?" Nolan asks as he sets a box labeled *shit that's going to expire soon* on the kitchen counter. "I was thinking pizza or Chinese."

"Oh god, yes *please*. I am starving."

"Pizza okay?"

I nod. "Fine by me."

"Topping preferences? Please don't say onions."

"Meat. Lots of it. The more, the better."

Nolan's brows shoot up at my words, and a wolfish grin curves his lips. "Well, we don't have to order pizza for that."

Huh? I...

Oh god.

My cheeks heat under his scrutiny, and I drop my head into my hands. "Ugh, I sound like such a hussy. I swear I'm not usually like this."

He chuckles. "It's fine. We can chalk it up to your tiredness."

"Thank you. I'll order the pizza."

"Yes, I'd rather they take that order from you than me."

"What? Not secure enough in your sexuality to place that one?"

"Oh, I'm secure. I just don't think I can get that out without laughing."

I shake my head, pulling my phone from my pocket with a grin.

There's a text waiting from Sam.

#1 Kid: Dad got me a new headset for my PS!

A pang of envy hits me.

Patrick's out taking Sam shopping while I'm moving us into someone else's apartment.

Me: Awesome!

#1 Kid: Yeah, and he got me new Nikes.

Probably the ones I couldn't afford for Christmas.

Me: How cool! Tell Dad I said hi.

#1 Kid: He says hi back.

Me: Love you, kiddo.

He sends me back a heart emoji.

"What has you smiling?"

"Huh?" I pull my attention from my phone. "Oh. Sam. He

was telling me about all the great things his dad is buying him."

"You don't sound happy about that."

I shrug. "It's fine."

Nolan levels me with a stare, begging for me to not lie to him.

I sigh. "Fine—it's not fine. It's actually really damn irritating because Patrick *knows* I don't make as much money as he does."

"You feel like he's rubbing it in your face?"

"Yes and no. I mean, it's not intentional. It's just not… thoughtful either, you know?"

"Have you told him how it makes you feel?"

I snort. "No. It's pointless. I spent the first several years of our marriage telling him how I felt, and it fell on deaf ears. It was how our relationship worked. I gave, he took. I tried, he didn't."

"That's shitty."

"It is, and it's a big reason we got divorced. I needed more, and I never got it. We didn't work together in the right areas."

"Why'd you stay married so long then?"

I pull my bottom lip between my teeth.

It's the question I ask myself all the time. If I wasn't happy, why did I stay for so damn long? Why did I try to force myself to love someone who didn't love me back?

It always comes back to the same answer—Sam.

"Sorry. It's none of my business," he says quickly.

"For Sam," I answer him anyway.

A frown pulls at his mouth, but he doesn't say anything else.

And I drop the subject.

Nolan doesn't need to hear about my marital problems of the past. I've moved on from it, so there's no reason to rehash it now.

Instead, I pull up the number to a pizza place nearby that delivers and get our order in for a large meat lovers pie and an order of breadsticks.

I excuse myself to my bedroom and get to work unpacking what little I brought with me. It's not much, mostly clothes and a few other essentials. I decided I would go light on this stay. Since I don't plan on us being here long, there was no need to haul all my stuff here.

I get so lost hanging up my work clothes that I don't even hear Nolan knock on my door, and I yelp when he speaks.

"Shit." I grab my chest, trying to calm my racing heart. "You scared the crap out of me."

"Sorry." Except he doesn't appear so. "Pizza's here."

"Oh, good. Let me grab my money."

"Already took care of it." He walks out of the room, and I follow him.

"You should have let me pay," I say to his back.

"It's not a big deal."

"I don't need you buying everything for me. I see you didn't bother listening to me about the bathroom stuff either. I want to pay you back for that too."

"Nah."

"Nolan." I yank on his shirt to stop him.

He spins around to face me, and suddenly he's right there. So incredibly close.

That same fresh mountain air scent hits me.

It has to be his body wash. There's no way a person just smells this good.

"It is."

"Huh?" I glance up at him. "What?"

He smirks down at me. "It's my body wash."

Oh crap...

"Look," he says, brushing past my embarrassment, "buying the bathroom stuff isn't a big deal. Buying breakfast isn't a big deal. The pizza isn't one either."

"Don't forget you bought me drinks too."

"I thought we were both supposed to forget about that."

"Right. No harm, no foul, yeah?"

The words sound snippy even to my ears, and I wish I could take them back because Nolan was right. We should forget about that night.

Besides, nothing happened.

I mean, it would have, but it didn't. So it's no big deal, right?

He tips his head to the side, studying me.

His penetrating gaze has me shifting on my feet.

I sigh. "I don't want you to keep thinking I'm some sort of charity case who needs someone to rescue her all the time. I'm perfectly capable of taking care of myself. I know you have a soft spot because your dad went through something similar, but I'm not him, okay?"

I've felt trapped and helpless in a relationship before, and I don't want to feel that again. Sure, this isn't a relationship, but the principle is the same.

When this is all said and done, I don't want to feel like I owe Nolan anything, and unlike when I walked away from my marriage, I'd like to come out the other side of this with my pride still intact.

His lips pull into a hard line like he's annoyed, but I can't tell whether it's at me or himself.

Finally, he nods once. "Okay."

"Okay. Thank you." I blow out a breath. "Can we go eat pizza now? I'm starving."

Chapter 8

NOLAN

As annoyed as I was with Maya about how upset she was about me buying a few things, I'm more annoyed with myself because I dared to give a shit in the first place. Inserting myself into her life, simply buying things for her, is opening too many doors for me to get sucked through and end up attached to her, and I can't afford that.

I'm already treading in dangerous territory allowing her to stay here when I find her so damn attractive, never mind she's barely been my tenant for a full twelve hours and I've already opened up to her more than I have to anyone other than Dean.

I've always been careful about how close I get to anyone, and in a matter of hours, she's already torn down too many barriers.

Like when I found myself getting jealous of her being all smiley with Cooper. Which was fucking ridiculous on my part.

One, he's with Caroline. He has no interest in Maya.

Two, Maya is nobody but my new temporary roommate. That's it.

And I need to keep reminding myself of that.

She'll be gone soon, like everyone else. No reason to let my guard down, no matter how much I want to kiss her.

With a huff, I punch my pillow and roll over for the millionth time in the last thirty minutes. Usually, I have no problem passing out once I click off my TV for the night, but I can't fucking sleep for shit right now.

And I'm pretty sure it has everything to do with the beauty across the hall.

I need a distraction, something to ease my mind.

I need a book.

Problem is, everything is in my library.

Where Maya is.

I close my eyes, trying to force myself to sleep and clear my mind, but another ten minutes pass and it's still not working because all I can think about is how cute Maya looked hauling boxes into the back of my truck today.

She didn't sit there and let me do all the work like the women I've been with in the past would have. Hell, I think she was actually a little pissed I called Cooper to help.

She's independent and hates relying on anyone else.

It's one of the things I like about her.

The apartment is quiet, so I hear the soft click of the door across the hall when it's opened.

Oh, thank god.

As soon as I hear the bathroom door closing, I make my move.

I toss my blanket off, swing out of my bed, and rush across the hall into the darkened room. I don't bother turning on the light. There's no need with the soft glow of the moon pouring in through the window.

I notice the two open boxes sitting in the corner alongside a suitcase, and a frown tugs at my lips.

When I walked into her apartment earlier, I wasn't ready for it to be so bare. She's only here for a couple of months, but surely she's not expecting to live out of boxes that entire time?

Whatever. Not my problem.

With a shake of my head, I go to the bookshelf full of my favorites and retrieve a copy of *The Hobbit*. It's a long read, but an easy one to get sucked into…I hope.

In case it doesn't work, I grab two other books.

As quietly as I can, I make my way out of the room, pulling her door back to where it was so she doesn't know I was ever in here. The last thing I need is for her to think I'm some creeper riffling through her panties.

The bathroom door is pulled open and shut and then a tiny body is running into me.

Maya screams.

The next thing I know, my books are on the floor and she's pressed against the wall with my hand over her mouth.

And I fucking feel her everywhere.

I'm trying hard as hell to not react to the way her breasts keep brushing against my naked chest…or how I can feel her hardened nipples through her shirt.

My other hand is holding on to her waist, my fingers tightly gripping on. My leg is pressed between her thighs, and it's painfully obvious she's not wearing any pants.

Oh god. How the fuck did we end up like this?

She swallows against me, and the recognition slowly enters her wild eyes. Only then do I remove my hand.

"Holy fuck," she mutters, gulping in air. "I totally forgot you live here too."

I chuckle. "It's my apartment."

"Right, right." She gulps. "Right."

"You okay?" I ask in a whisper as I trace my thumb over her soft cheek.

I should stop touching her, but I can't seem to make myself do it.

She nods. "I think so." Then she lets out a laugh that's not full of much humor. "Fuck."

"I didn't mean to scare you."

Her tongue darts out to wet her lips, and I track the movement with my eyes. "What were you doing in my room?"

I read every word that comes out of her mouth since I'm still staring at her lips.

I need to *stop* staring at her lips.

She's too close right now, and I'm too worried I'm not going to be able to stop myself from doing something stupid.

Like kiss her.

I drag my eyes from her pretty, perfect mouth, but staring into her eyes isn't much better.

Fuck.

"Couldn't sleep," I explain as she stares at me expectantly. "I needed something to read."

"Oh." She sounds relieved, yet somehow still disappointed.

I can't help but laugh. "Is that not the answer you expected?"

She swallows. "No. It's just…" She trails off, her teeth

sinking into her plump bottom lip as she darts her eyes away from me.

It hits me: she thought I was in there for something else.

She thought I was in there for *her*.

The desire I've been pushing down since the moment I saw her sitting at the bar races through me, and, unable to stop myself, I dip my head toward her, those lips that are begging to be kissed a mere inch away.

I'm so damn close I smell the minty freshness of her toothpaste, and part of me wonders if she tastes like it too.

My lips curve into a smile as I gaze into her gray eyes that may be my undoing. "Did you want me to be there for a different reason, Maya?"

"W-What? N-No."

She gulps again, then wiggles against me, and it's a painful reminder that she's not wearing any pants as her pussy brushes against my thigh. Her eyes widen the second we make contact.

A small moan escapes, and as if she can't help it, she moves again.

And then again.

She's practically humping my leg, and I can't seem to make myself want her to stop.

But we should.

Before something happens we can't take back.

Except another soft whimper hits my ears, and before I know it, I'm capturing it with my mouth.

Time stills when our lips press together. It's soft and chaste.

Then, all at once, we explode.

We're so frenzied our teeth gnash together with urgency,

and her fingers curl into my shoulders, pulling me to her like she's been dying for me to kiss her.

She rubs her pussy against my thigh again, and I swallow another moan, curling my fingers into her long, dark locks and tilting her head until I get the access I'm dying for.

I run my tongue along the seam of her lips, and she opens for me without hesitation.

Our tongues clash, creating a rhythm all their own.

My hand moves from her waist to her ass, pulling her tighter to me, helping her as she rocks her hips against me. There's no mistaking the wet spot forming on my pajama bottoms.

She's getting herself off on my thigh, and I'm happy as fuck to oblige.

I want to see her come.

I pull my lips from her, nipping my way across her jaw and down her neck, then back up again.

Her panting grows louder with each stroke against me as she inches closer to where she needs to be.

"Do it," I say. "Get yourself there."

My words snap her out of the haze she's in, and she's no longer pulling me closer, but pushing me away.

I don't overstay my welcome, putting some space between us until I can see what's happening.

And what's happening is the storm brewing in her eyes.

She's upset, but I can tell it's not with me.

"No," she mutters, slamming her eyes closed. "No, no, no." She lifts her lids again, that fucking gray stare penetrating me. "We can't."

We…can't?

Oh fuck.

We *can't*.

I push away from her, not stopping until I'm safely on the other side of the hall because I can't think clearly when I'm near her.

She flattens herself against the wall, tipping her head up, sucking in several deep breaths while I do the same.

What the hell am I thinking? What the hell am I *doing*?

We can't get into this together.

She's not some random girl I met at the bar. She's not some chick I met on an app for a hookup.

She's my roommate.

She's River's best friend.

She's a mom.

Attachment after attachment after *fucking* attachment.

We can*not* do this.

It's too risky.

"I'm sorry," she murmurs. "I shouldn't have let things go so far."

"Don't." I shake my head. "It's my fault. I'm the one who initiated it."

"But I didn't stop it," she argues.

Fine. If she wants part of the blame, she can have it.

We stand there for several minutes longer. Or hours. I can't really tell at this point.

Maya is the first to move.

She bends, grabbing my three dropped—and long-forgotten—books off the floor. The pages are bent, but it's nothing a bit of weight can't straighten out.

She takes a step toward me. "I'm sorry about your books."

I shrug, pushing off the wall and meeting her in the

middle. "It's fine. Books are meant to be read and beat up a little bit. That's what they're there for."

She nods, and her eyes drop to my lips, like she's considering kissing me again. I watch the turmoil work its way through her gaze until there's nothing there but resolve.

Resolve that we can't do this.

She pushes her shoulders back and lifts her chin, then holds the books out to me. I stare at them a beat before I accept them, not wanting to accept that this is for the best.

But we both know it is.

We move carefully, ensuring our fingertips don't brush during the exchange.

She takes a steadying breath, then nods again before moving toward her room.

I grab her wrist.

I don't fucking know why I grab her wrist.

She glances down to where my fingers are encircling her, then her eyes flit to mine.

They're questioning, and I don't have the answers.

Instead, I swipe my thumb over the inside of her wrist.

"Good night, Juliet."

One side of her lips tips up. "Good night, Romeo."

And somehow, with all the willpower in the world, I let her go.

The next day is every bit as awkward as I lay in bed imagining it would be.

Maya's sitting on one side of the kitchen counter, sipping a glass of wine to go along with the pasta dish she cooked up.

I'm standing as far away from her as I can get, practically in the corner of the kitchen like a kid who's done something bad and awaits a punishment.

"Thank you for the creamer." She takes another drink from her glass.

I went to the store the night before she moved in and made sure I had enough food to get us by until we could figure out a grocery schedule. I remembered she used vanilla creamer in her coffee at The Gravy Train, so I made sure to grab a container of it.

"Welcome."

"And for the muffins this morning."

I barely slept last night after we went our separate ways and was up well before my alarm clock went off. Normally I'd whip up a few eggs and toast for breakfast, but I didn't want to risk waking Maya up, so I ran down to the diner and grabbed something quick.

"No problem," I tell her.

Because it wasn't. If I hadn't left, I'd have probably done something stupid like crawl into bed with her.

The walk to the diner helped clear my head.

Last night was a big mistake, one we can't let happen again—one I don't intend on letting happen again. From here on out, we're strictly roommates.

"Do you not like the pasta?"

"Huh?"

She nods toward the bowl I'm holding in my hand. "You've hardly touched it. I figured you'd be starving after being out all day. If it's not good, that's okay too. I told you I know my way around the kitchen a bit, but it doesn't mean all my dishes are hits."

I was starving…until I remembered I had to come home to Maya in my apartment.

"It's delicious." A frown pulls at her lips like she doesn't believe me. "No, really. See?" I shove a giant forkful into my mouth, chew, then swallow.

It truly is good. Probably one of the best dishes I've ever had.

My father tried his hardest to do what he could in the kitchen when my mom left, but he never quite got the hang of it. More nights than not, we ate sandwiches or macaroni and cheese.

"I'm tired is all," I explain. "I zone out a bit when I get that way. I'm not trying to not eat."

She looks like she wants to say something else but decides against it. Instead, she nods, then drops her attention back to the bowl in front of her, which is almost as full as mine.

I shovel several more bites of the tomatoey pasta into my gullet to make her happy, then reach for the can of soda I have sitting on the counter next to me and take a drink.

Her fork clatters against the bowl, and I nearly spit my drink out, caught off guard.

She turns her fiery eyes to me. "Are we going to talk about last night or sit in awkward silence for the rest of the time I'm living here?"

"Nope," I tell her. I finish off the rest of my soda, then crush the can against my leg and toss it into the trash can across from me.

She huffs out a growl. "Why not?"

"Because nothing happened."

"Nolan, come on." She sighs. "Be an adult about this."

"I am. I'm moving on and you should too."

Her eyes sharpen on me again and she works her jaw back and forth. "Really?"

"Yup."

"Fine," she snips back.

I drop my fork into my now empty bowl, then march to the sink. I rinse out the dirty dish and plop it into the dishwasher.

I can feel her eyes on me as I grab the plug from under the sink and put it in place. I twist on the hot water and squirt out some dish soap, letting it fill up while I grab the dirty pots and pans from the stovetop.

She doesn't say anything as she finishes off her dinner and drains the rest of her wine…then refills it with well over two fingers of bourbon.

Without another word, glass in hand, she pads down the hall to her bedroom.

She doesn't slam the door, and somehow that's worse.

Somehow, I know it means she's truly pissed.

Good. Let her be angry.

Anger will keep her away.

Anger will keep us separated.

Anger will keep me from making any more dumb decisions.

I don't need to get involved with Maya for a myriad of reasons, the biggest being I can't give her what she wants the most—love.

Chapter 9

MAYA

Moving in with Nolan was a massive mistake for one obvious reason: I'm undeniably attracted to him.

Based on that alone, I should have thanked him politely for his offer and declined it, then moved in with River and Dean.

Except I couldn't do that. I couldn't put them through that.

So I pulled up my big girl panties and moved in with the first guy to make me want to pull said panties down in a *long* time.

We've barely talked since we kissed. We've been too busy tiptoeing around one another to speak.

Luckily, Nolan works long hours, so I only have to avoid him in the evenings when he's home. I make dinner and leave it on the stove for him, then hide away in my bedroom. I've already blazed through two whole seasons of *Dawson's Creek*, so I can't say it's been a total waste.

"So, how's everything going with Nolan? I feel like we haven't had a real chance to talk this week with all the orders coming into the shop." River shovels a bite of pie into her mouth. How she can eat that many sweets, especially in the morning, is beyond me, but the girl can consume pie like nobody's business.

It's Sunday morning and we're at The Gravy Train for our near-weekly routine of breakfast and gossip. Though, admittedly, it's not as much fun as it used to be back when River was single and dating. Now, we mostly complain about customers at work.

"It's fine."

Her fork stops mid-bite, and she tips her head to the side. I shift under her watchful gaze, hating the way she's staring at me. "You keep saying that, but I'm not sure you mean it."

My heart rate picks up. Does she know about the kiss? No, that's crazy. There's no way she could.

"What do you mean?" I ask, playing it cool.

She stabs her utensil my way. "I've known you twenty-plus years. You've been crazy distracted at work this week, and you look like you haven't slept much. So, something must have happened."

Yeah, I kissed Nolan!

I want to yell it across the table so badly…but not as badly as I want to kiss him again.

It's all I've been able to think about. No matter the number of times I run my fingers over my clit, nothing feels as good as it did when Nolan's leg was between my thighs.

I clear my throat, squeezing my legs together at the memory.

"Nothing happened," I lie.

I hate lying to her, but I don't want to tell River about the kiss because she's going to think it means something, and it definitely does *not* mean anything.

It can't. She told me herself Nolan doesn't date. Hell, *he* told me too. He doesn't do relationships, and he definitely doesn't do kids.

Us kissing? Doesn't mean a thing because nothing will ever come from it, so there's no reason to tell her if it doesn't mean anything.

At least that's what I'm telling myself.

"I'm still…adjusting," I add.

She nods. "I'm sure it's all a little strange still. But like I said, Nolan's a cool guy, and you guys will get along great."

Don't blush. Don't blush. Do not blush.

"I'm sure we will. He's not home a lot, so we haven't spent much time together." Because we've been ignoring one another, but she doesn't know that.

"You two should come down for dinner one night. Just us adults. We can get shit-faced without having to worry about anyone driving home."

It's an awful idea.

It's awkward enough when we're alone. I can't imagine how much worse it would be if we had to pretend I didn't almost get myself off on him in front of other people.

"I'll talk to Dean and see what night works for him," she continues. "Maybe we'll do a Sunday, that way we won't have to worry about opening the boutique hungover."

I smile but don't say anything.

Luckily, my phone buzzes against the table before she can keep pressing the subject.

#1 Kid: Dad wants to know if you can pick me up early today??

I try not to be annoyed it's Sam texting me and not his father. Patrick always makes Sam be the one to contact me.

Ridiculous because the man always has his phone attached to his ear. I know he knows how to use it just fine.

Me: You know I'm always ready for you to come home. But what's up?

#1 Kid: He says he has a lunch meeting he forgot about in Jonesville at 12 and has to leave soon.

"What's up?" River asks. "Sam?"

"Yeah. Patrick needs me to come get him early."

She glances at the time on her phone. "That's fine. I can cover the boutique by myself for a bit."

Oh crap. My shift. That means Sam will be home most of the day alone with Nolan.

I mean, they have to spend time together sometime, right? I just hoped it wouldn't be so soon.

Me: That's fine. I'll leave now.

#1 Kid: Dad says thanks.

I try not to roll my eyes. *Of course he does.* I'm picking up his slack yet again.

"Well, I guess breakfast is over then." I push my plate across the table, then reach into my purse. I toss five bucks on the table for Darlene. "I need to get back to the apartment and change so I can head straight to the store once I pick him up."

"Don't worry about it," River reassures me as I hop off my stool. "Take your time. I'm sure you're dying to see your kiddo anyway."

I really am.

As glad as I am Patrick and I were able to work out a custody arrangement, I miss Sam so much when he spends a week at his father's.

"Thank you," I tell her. I round the table and press a kiss to her cheek. "You're the best."

"I know. Tell my asshole nephew I don't forgive him for that move he pulled last night."

"Huh?"

She lifts her phone. "Little twerp sent his clan to attack me when my old ass was sleeping. He nearly cost me the game."

I laugh. Sometimes I forget River plays some game with Sam. They've been battling each other for like two years now. "I can't believe you're still playing with him."

"I'll play until one of us perishes."

My eyes widen.

"In the game!" she amends, laughing. Then she shoos me away. "Go get your hellion."

"Son of a…" I stomp my foot against the hard concrete, ignoring the pain shooting up my leg. "You have to be freakin' kidding me!"

My words echo around the parking garage as I stare down at the flat tire I have.

"Things couldn't go right for more than one week, could they?" I mutter to nobody but myself.

It's a Sunday and all the repair shops are closed, which sucks because of course I never replaced my spare from the last time I had a flat tire.

I toss my head back with a groan.

Normally if something like this were to happen, I'd call River, but since she's at work covering my shift…well, I'm screwed.

I can call Patrick and let him know I can't pick up Sam

early, but he'll just be a dick about it, even though *I'm* the one doing *him* a favor.

"Well, that's a bummer," comes a smooth voice from next to me.

I slam my eyes closed and take a deep breath, wishing I were anywhere but here.

"What are you doing down here?"

"Was gonna take a drive." He jingles his keys in front of him. "Been cooped up in the apartment too long and need a breather. Didn't feel like walking, wanted to roll the windows down and cruise."

I nod, understanding him more than he knows.

Eager to have a reason to get out of the apartment this morning, I was a half hour early to meet River, and that *never* happens.

"Do you have a spare?"

"No." I sigh. "I've been meaning to replace it, but I just… haven't."

"It's a good thing we don't live too far from stuff then."

He's right. His apartment is in a popular shopping district and pretty much everything—including Sam's school—is within walking distance. So even if I have to wait a few days to get the tire changed, I'll be fine.

Except for right now when I need to be somewhere.

"Do you want a ride?"

"No."

He laughs. "Let me rephrase that. Do you *need* a ride?"

I want to say no. I want to be able to walk away and take care of my own problems.

But I can't.

Again.

"Are we talking all of a sudden?"

He doesn't answer right away, and we stand there staring at the flat tire for several quiet seconds.

"We're not *not* talking." I smile at his non-answer. "Is that a yes on the ride?"

"Please."

He nods, then leads the way across the parking garage to his truck. It annoys me when I see he's backed into the spot like some show-off.

We climb into the big vehicle and Nolan fires up the engine.

"Where to?" he asks, peeking over at me.

"White Wing Estates. I have to pick up Sam from his father's."

"Ah." He nods, throwing the truck into drive and inching out of the parking space. "I thought his father had him until this evening?"

"Patrick had a work thing come up." There's a tic in his jaw, though I'm not sure what it means. I have a feeling even if I asked, he wouldn't answer. "If you're serious about the ride, you can drop us off at Making Waves for my shift."

His thick, dark brows slam together, and his lips that I know are softer than they look twist up. "Why would you need to take him to work with you?"

"Because otherwise he'd be at the apartment with you pretty much all day."

"And you don't trust him with me?"

"No. I just know you hate kids."

He sighs, his grip tightening on the wheel as he grits his teeth. "If I didn't want your son at my apartment, I wouldn't have offered up my rooms to you, okay?"

I've never heard him so frustrated before.

But I guess I don't understand him, don't understand why he's offered up his place to a single mom when he doesn't like kids and clearly doesn't want me there.

When I don't answer him, he glances over at me.

"Okay?" he presses again, his voice and eyes softer this time.

"Okay."

"Good."

He flips on the radio, and the sounds of seventies and eighties rock fill the silence.

Even though we're not spending much time together, the sexual tension between us is still palpable.

He looks at me, and I look away.

I glance at him, and he does the same.

Back and forth and back and forth.

It's exhausting, and I want things to not be awkward again. I don't want this silence stretching between us now to last the whole time I'm in his apartment. I can't stomach it much longer.

When we trek closer to my old neighborhood, I steer him through the streets until he's parking in front of Patrick's two-story house.

"I'll leave the engine running."

With a nod, I hop out of the car, walk the short path to the front door, and knock.

Patrick swings the door open, his face pulled tight.

"Oh, thank god it's you. I have to leave ASAP if I want to make my lunch meeting."

"Should have thought about that more than an hour ago, Patrick," I remind him not-so-gently.

He huffs. "It was a calendar mistake, okay? It's not my fault."

He means it's his secretary's.

A part of me wondered if he was sleeping with her when we were together, but honestly, by the time we got divorced, I didn't care anymore. We might have been married on paper, but we hadn't been *married* for a long time when we ended things.

"Your son ready?"

"Oh, so now he's my son, huh?" He grins at me, and for a moment I see the boy I fell for at sixteen. But as quickly as he appears, he's gone again. "Sammy!" he hollers up the stairs. "Mom's here!"

"Coming!" he calls back.

Patrick turns to me and sighs. "Look, sorry. I didn't want to cut our weekend short, but this meeting is important. I can't miss it or my dad will have my ass."

I nod, having known his apology was coming before he even started. It's what he does. "It's fine."

It's not, but we'll talk about it later when Sam's not lurking around the corner.

"Where's your car?" he asks, realizing my little Honda isn't in the driveway.

"Flat tire. I got a ride from a friend."

He slides his eyes past me toward where Nolan's parked on the curb.

"That the roommate Sammy told me about?"

I glance over my shoulder, peeking back at Nolan, who's watching us with curious eyes.

He looks ready to pounce out of the truck at any moment, and I appreciate that he's there to have my back if I need it.

Though Patrick can be a dick at times, Nolan doesn't need to worry. I can handle him myself.

"Yep."

"You didn't tell me you were moving in with some guy, Maya." He doesn't sound jealous—probably because he knows better—but he does sound worried.

"It's just temporary," I explain. "I'm waiting on a new-build apartment to open up leasing."

"I wish you would have come to me before you moved in with a stranger."

"That's not your job anymore, Patrick."

His mouth opens like he wants to argue that point, then he snaps it back closed with a nod, realizing it's moot.

"Besides," I continue, "Nolan isn't a stranger. He's best friends with River's boyfriend."

"Ah, yes. Mr. Evans." He clears his throat. *"He's, like, the coolest teacher ever, Dad,"* he mocks in Sam's high-pitched puberty whine.

I laugh. "Yep, the one and only."

"Do you think Sammy likes him more than me?"

"Shit, I think he likes him more than *me*, and we both know I'm the favorite parent."

There's the briefest flash of hurt in Patrick's eyes, and I wonder for a moment if there's something he's not telling me. It vanishes just as fast though, and he laughs at my joke.

He clears his throat. "You really should get a house, you know. Apartment living is for the birds, and the market isn't awful right now. I bet you could find something on your budget."

He doesn't mean for the words to sting, but they do anyway.

"I'm fine with apartment living for now, thank you." I'm not, but I don't want him to know that. "It's nice to see you still worry about me."

"You're the mother of my favorite son. I'll always worry about you."

"Hey! I'm your only son," Sam says, ambling down the stairs, carrying much more than he came here with.

My first instinct is to scold Patrick for buying him so much stuff, but it's another conversation for another time.

"You ready?" I ask him, reaching for a bag so he can hug his dad.

"Yep."

"I'm heading out now, too," Patrick says, grabbing his briefcase from the spot by the door where he always keeps it and following us onto the porch.

I look away as Patrick wraps him in a hug, letting them have this moment together.

As much as I wish Patrick would put his phone down or make his time with Sam a priority a little more often, there is absolutely no doubt in my mind that he loves his son more than anything in the world.

One of the few times I've seen him cry was when I asked for a divorce. It wasn't because our marriage was ending, but because he was scared I would take Sam away from him.

He never had to worry about that though.

"See you later, Sammy," he says, then he leans toward me and presses a kiss to my cheek. "I'll call you sometime this week."

I nod, fighting the urge to wipe off his kiss. It's not something new. He always kisses my cheek, but somehow him doing it in front of Nolan feels wrong.

Which is ridiculous as hell. Nolan is nobody but my roommate.

"Bye, Patrick." I usher Sam off the porch as Patrick heads for his brand-new coupe.

"Did you have fun at your dad's?" I ask Sam as we make our way back to Nolan's truck.

He bobs his head. "We played laser tag Friday night and I whooped his ass."

"Your dad was always awful at laser tag." I should probably get on to him for cussing, but he doesn't do it often, so I let it slide.

"You've played him before?"

"Yep. Our first date. I, too, whooped his ass."

He laughs as we pile into Nolan's truck as Patrick pulls out of the driveway. Nolan watches the car as it passes by us, then he peeks over at me.

"Good?"

I nod.

He turns around to Sam and puts his fist out for a bump. "'Sup, shithead?"

"Hey, Nolan."

They clash their knuckles together, then Nolan turns back around, puts the car in drive, and starts down the road.

"Did you just call my son a shithead?"

"Yep." He says it so matter-of-factly, and I grin, loving how he doesn't back down even though I am definitely giving him my best mom stare right now.

"And why is he a shithead?"

"Because when Dean nailed me in the nuts with the football, your son laughed for ten minutes straight, then proceeded to make fun of me because I allegedly cried."

I lift a brow. "Well, did you?"

"Hell yes I cried! Have you ever been sacked in the nuts with a football flying through the air at like forty miles per hour?"

I snicker. "Can't say I have."

"Exactly, so pipe down over there, no-nuts."

"Yeah, Mom," Sam says, "if you don't have nuts, you don't get a say."

"Can we leave my nonexistent nuts out of this?" I glance between the two of them. "I'm feeling very ganged up on right now."

They shrug in unison, and I grin.

"Nolan, do you play video games?"

"I'm really good at Mario Kart," he answers.

Sam grins. "We'll get along just fine then."

He then slides his attention to his phone, and we ride in silence for another couple of miles.

"You good?" Nolan asks out of the side of his mouth, so low and quiet I barely hear him.

What he's really asking: *Are* we *good?*

He doesn't want things to be awkward between us anymore, and I don't either. I just want to move on and spend the rest of the next two months without worry.

"Yep. You?"

He nods. "Golden like a shower."

"What's a golden shower?" Sam pipes up from the back seat. I didn't even realize he was paying any attention to us.

I bury my face in my hands, mortified my son just asked about a golden shower.

"It's when you dump apple juice on someone you don't like," Nolan answers, not appearing the least bit fazed.

"Oh. Then why are you like one?"

"It's an expression for being happy."

"Ah, I understand now. You're so happy because you finally stood up to a bully." He snaps his fingers together. "Man, I should give Jaxson a golden shower. He's always being a jerk. He deserves it."

"Oh my god," I mutter to Nolan. "I hate you so much."

His body quakes with laughter and he shakes his head. "Good save though, huh? Gotta remember there are little ears around."

He doesn't seem annoyed by Sam and his naivety.

Instead, he looks amused, like he's looking forward to what the kid might say next.

All my worries about Sam and Nolan spending time together fly out the window.

Chapter 10

NOLAN

"Nolan, you home?"

"Yeah!"

The front door latches into place and Maya's shoes smack against the hardwood floor as she makes her way through the apartment to where I'm at in my library.

"What are you doing in here?"

"Looking for a new book. Finished mine." I hold up the paperback I finished last night.

Rain started pouring early this morning and the jobsite was shut down, so I now have the rest of the day off. With it still dumping rain, I don't have much else to do besides read.

"This is my room."

"I'm aware." She narrows her eyes, and I sigh, focusing my attention back on my shelves. "I promise I didn't touch your unmentionables, and I definitely didn't see the bra hanging on the closet door handle."

Her cheeks heat and she rushes into the room to remove the bra from my sight, swinging open the door of the closet and chucking it in, then slamming it back closed.

She's too late though. It's already burned into my brain.

I've tried to not spend a lot of time wondering what Maya's wearing underneath the clothes I so fucking desperately want to peel off her, but I wasn't expecting the sexy, pink, lace-covered bra.

I've been staring at this shelf for the last ten minutes because I can't stop thinking about if the panties match.

Fuck do I hope they match.

I push the thought aside because I shouldn't be having it at all.

But I can't seem to stop myself.

We've fallen into a sort of rhythm over the last week. We're no longer ignoring one another, but we're not suddenly best friends either. It also hasn't escaped me that Maya has done everything in her power to ensure we're never alone in the same room together.

We're just…co-existing.

Which is fine. It's what I wanted. No skin off my back.

"Can I ask why you're screaming my name across the apartment? I don't usually make women yell unless it's in the bedroom…" I slide my eyes toward her bed, smirking. "Oh. Look. A bed."

She huffs, but I don't miss the way her eyes find the bed too. She snaps them back to me just as fast. "Tell me it wasn't you."

"It wasn't me."

She clenches her teeth. "Nolan…"

"What?"

"My tire—did you fix it?"

"Oh. That. Yeah, I did."

"Why?"

She's a friend, right? Friends can help friends.

Or at least that's what I told myself when I showed up to the parking garage with a shiny new tire and a jack.

I shrug, grabbing another book from the shelf, flipping it over to read the back. A lot of my shelves are lined with books I haven't yet read. "You needed a tire, and I had some time."

She pinches the bridge of her nose between her fingers. "I thought we talked about you doing stuff like that. I'm not your—"

"Charity case. Yeah, I heard you." I settle on two new books, then tuck them into my hand, pushing myself up to my full height. "But you're my tenant. If you don't work, I don't get paid. I was doing it for me, not you."

We both know that's bullshit since her shop isn't far from here and she walks most days anyway. I pray she doesn't call me out on it.

She's frustrated, but I can tell she doesn't want to argue.

Thank fuck for that. I'm not in the mood either. All I want to do is relax and read for a bit, maybe finish the true crime documentary I started.

"Well, thank you," she murmurs. "I suppose."

"You're welcome…I suppose."

Her lips twitch. "What are you doing home right now anyway? I saw your truck in the garage when I was on my way up and wondered."

"Rain delay. It's not looking like it's going to let up anytime soon, so we're off the rest of the day."

"Ah."

"What are you doing here?"

I rake my eyes over her outfit. She's not dressed for work,

and I know that because her work attire usually includes a pair of jeans that show off her curves in ways I can't ignore. But today she's—

Oh, fuck me.

No wonder her bra was hanging on the door—she's not fucking wearing one.

Like she can feel my eyes, her nipples form stiff peaks, and I have to fight the urge to cross the room and see if the color of them matches those pink lips I know taste sweeter than sin.

My dick jumps to life behind the zipper of my jeans.

Look away, Nolan. Just fucking look away. She's off limits.

"I'm off today," she says, drawing my eyes away from her chest. "I walked down to The Gravy Train for coffee, then stopped at the grocery store for bread before it really started coming down. I was going to make some of the soup I spotted in the pantry and a grilled cheese for a late lunch. You interested?"

As if on cue, my stomach growls.

She laughs. "I'll take that as a yes."

"I don't say no to a home-cooked meal very often."

She crinkles her nose up. "It's not really home-cooked. I'm just cracking open a can."

"Are you making it on the stove and not in the microwave?" She nods. "Then it's home-cooked enough for me." I head for the door. "You coming?"

"I'll be out there in a sec. Gonna change. I'm wet."

I raise my brow.

"From the rain," she clarifies with wide eyes.

I chuckle, then head for my room, where I swap my jeans

for sweats. It's a rainy day, and rainy days mean bumming around in sweats.

When she meets me in the kitchen a few minutes later, she's wearing a pair of black leggings with a few holes in them and a sweater about three sizes too big, the sleeves rolled up on her forearms. Her hair is now twisted into one of those messy buns, and she somehow looks about five years younger.

"Tomato or chicken noodle?" she asks, pushing her sleeves up higher.

"Your pick," I tell her, watching her stretch to reach the top shelf of the pantry.

The sweater she's wearing rides up with the movement, and someone ought to tell her those leggings are see-through when she does that, but it sure as hell won't be me. I like the sight far too much.

I look away before my cock starts to respond. The last thing I need is for her to glance over here and see me rocking a half-chub.

"We'll do tomato then." She pads out of the pantry, closing the door behind her. "I really only like to have canned chicken noodle if I'm in a pinch."

"You make it homemade?"

"Yep." She shoos me out of the way and grabs a pot from the cabinet beside the stove, then flips the burner on. She shoves the can of soup my way. "Open that, please."

I retrieve the can opener from the drawer and crank the can open.

"It's simple, actually—the chicken noodle soup, I mean," she continues. "The hardest part is getting the seasoning just right. I've spent a lot of time perfecting it over the years, so I've got it down to a science now."

I dump the soup into the pot as she reaches into the spice cabinet.

"Oh, wow. This is kind of sad," she remarks, taking inventory of what little spices I have.

"I told you—I'm not much of a cook."

"I can see that." She slides some spices around, then pulls a few out and sets them on the counter. "Hmm. We can work with this. Want to start on the grilled cheese? If you can handle it, I mean." She grins.

I narrow my eyes at her. "I can make grilled cheese."

"I'll be the judge of that."

We work side by side, her dressing up the tomato soup and me making the best damn grilled cheese she'll ever have.

About ten minutes later, we're plating our food. She hops up onto the counter to eat, and I lean against the counter across from her.

I take a bite of the soup, and flavor explodes on my tongue.

I mean, it's just canned soup, but she really dressed it up.

"This is good."

"Right? Adding a few spices kicks things up a notch. Normally I'd add some chipotle into the mix, but you didn't have any."

"You a spicy food fan?"

"Oh yeah. The spicier the better."

"Like the meatier the better?"

Her cheeks redden, and I swear her eyes drop to my crotch for the briefest of seconds before she's clearing her throat and looking away.

"I should have brought my table and chairs too," she says. "That way we could eat at the table."

"Nah. You're only here two months, right? No sense hauling your stuff all over the place. Besides, I should get my own shit soon. I'm just awful at picking stuff out."

"Let me help then. Maybe the next time we're both off, we can go shopping?"

I should say no, should not let her get more tangled up in my life and continue keeping her at arm's length.

Instead, I find myself nodding. "Yeah, I'd like that."

"It's a date then."

I wait for the panic to hit me at her choice of words.

It never comes.

She sets her soup down, then picks up her grilled cheese and takes a healthy bite.

"Oh shit." She moans, and the sound goes straight to my dick. *Calm down, boy.* "This is so good, Nolan."

"It's just grilled cheese."

"It's damn good grilled cheese." She takes another bite, then swallows. "Man, I can't remember the last time someone cooked for me at home. Probably not since I lived with my parents."

"Did your ex not cook for you?"

She barks out a laugh. "No. Never."

"Wait…like *never* never? In all the years you were married…never?"

She shakes her head. "No. He worked all the time, so I was responsible for making dinner."

"That's a stupid fucking excuse."

"Huh?"

"He was your husband. Working all the time or not, he

should have at least made you dinner sometimes. It's not like you were at home all day sitting around with your thumb up your ass. You were taking care of the house and your kid. You deserved a break too."

She blinks up at me with wide glassy eyes.

I shift back and forth on my feet, uncomfortable under her gaze. "What?"

The corners of her lips tip up, and she shakes her head. "Nothing. I just...well, thank you."

"I don't need to be thanked for telling the truth."

And I don't. What her ex did...that's wrong.

I saw how hard my father worked to keep our little family going. If her ex-husband was as flaky then as he is now, I know she was working as hard to keep her family together.

She deserved better than what he gave her.

Her lips part, like she's going to say something else, then thinks better of it.

We're quiet as we finish our lunch, no sound other than our spoons scraping against the bowls.

When we're done, I collect the dirty dishes, rinse them, and drop them into the dishwasher.

"So," Maya says from her perch on the counter, "other than making a bomb-ass grilled cheese, any other talents I should know about?"

"I can vibrate my eyes."

"Shut up. No you can't."

"Can too. See?" I make my eyes shake back and forth, something I learned I could do at an early age and used to impress girls...until I realized I wasn't special and shitloads of people could do it.

She squints, stretching forward to see. "I don't see anything."

I cross the short space between us, and she leans forward again.

"See?" I do it again and she gasps, slapping at me playfully. "Told you."

"That's a neat little party trick. How'd you learn that?"

I shrug. "No idea, but ten-year-old me used to do it all the time to impress the ladies. Did it work?"

"It's not bad." She giggles, and her fingers flex against me.

I realize then her hand is still on my chest. I glance down to where she's touching me, and her fingers work against my muscle again, pinching at my shirt.

She does it again, and I gulp.

I should walk away. Put as much distance between us as possible.

But I don't.

Her mouth opens with a breathy gasp as I put my hand on her calf. Slowly, I trail my fingers up her leg. She doesn't take her eyes off my touch, and I don't take mine off hers. Not even when I skim my hand over her knee and up her thigh.

It's fucking ridiculous. It's a simple touch.

But it feels like so much more, especially when her fingers curl into my shirt and she drags me closer until I'm right between her legs.

She pinches her eyes shut tight, then exhales heavily, and I don't dare move, too afraid I'm going to spook her.

When she finally opens her eyes, she's staring right at me...and she's begging me to do the one thing I've been wanting to do for over a week straight now.

Kiss her.

I'm not dumb enough to let the opportunity pass me by.

I crash my lips to hers, and she melts into me, sighing like she's been waiting for this moment for a lifetime.

I close the last of the distance between us, curling one hand around her waist and sliding the other into her messy bun, dragging her to the edge of the counter. My cock brushes against her pussy and I swallow her moan.

Her hands fist my shirt, holding on to me like I'm holding on to her—desperately.

Our mouths move together in a slow kiss as we find a rhythm with our hips, rubbing against one another like horny teens.

I brush the pad of my finger against her skin where her shirt has ridden up. She's soft and warm and feels so damn good. I inch my way up under her shirt, skidding my fingers over her, loving the way her skin rises against my touch. I'm pleased to find she never put a bra on as I cup her tit, brushing my thumb across her nipple. She shudders at the touch and groans into my mouth again.

I do it again.

And again.

She's so responsive, and I want nothing more than to rip this fucking sweater from her body and bury my face between her tits.

A wet spot forms on my sweats. I don't know if it's from my leaking dick or her soaking through her leggings, and fuck if that thought doesn't take me closer to the edge.

If we don't stop soon, I'm going to embarrass myself.

Not wanting to stop touching her, I pull my lips from hers and nip my way over her jaw as she gulps in air. Her fingers are still wrapped up in my shirt, holding me tight like she's afraid to let go as she slowly rubs against me.

"Nolan…" She whispers my name as a plea, and right now I'll give in to anything she asks me. "I need…"

She doesn't have to say anything.

I know what she needs.

Because I fucking need it too.

Without thinking too hard about it, I break our contact long enough to pull her shirt over her head. Her hands are on me again the moment it's gone.

I stare down at her as she peers up at me with lustful eyes, her tits hanging out in all their glory.

And they are glorious, too, the pink of her nipples matching her lips like I thought they would.

She's gorgeous, even when she blushes under my watchful gaze.

I hold her stare as I trace a single finger over the hardened buds, and I'm rewarded with another shudder.

"Beautiful," I mutter before I give in and close my mouth around her.

She groans and clutches the back of my head, holding me to her, and I nearly come right then.

I switch to her other breast, nipping and lapping at the sensitive peaks. I don't know how long I spend going back and forth—I could do it all fucking day—but I don't miss the way her breathing stutters and she's writhing against the counter, searching for more contact.

I'm more than willing to oblige.

I trail kisses back to her lips, covering her whimpers with my mouth, and finger the waist of her leggings.

When she realizes what I'm wanting, she tips her hips toward me, more than eager for my touch.

I slip my fingers into the band and—

Ring! Ring! Ring!

Maya freezes.

And reality crashes back down around us.

With reluctance, I drag my mouth away from hers, the cold slamming into me as I step away from her warmth. My hands itch to hold her again, so I put as much space between us as possible, resting against the counter opposite her, working to catch my breath.

She sits wide-eyed, lips swollen from my kisses and topless. Her chest is rising and falling in quick succession, her face flushed from the orgasm she was on the verge of.

Her phone rings again, and she springs into action, racing across the apartment to answer it.

"Hello?" she says. "Oh, shit. Yes, okay. I'm on my way."

There's shuffling in the other room, and when she comes back out, she's wearing jeans and a new shirt.

"Sam forgot his project that's due next period..." she explains, heading for the door and pulling on her shoes. She slings her purse over her shoulder. When her hand falls to the doorknob, she pauses and glances at me. "Nolan, I..." She licks her lips. "I—"

"Go," I tell her. "We'll talk about it later."

Her teeth find her bottom lip again in the move that drives me wild, and she nods once.

Then, she's gone.

And I'm left wondering what the fuck we just did.

Something is happening, and I'm not sure how to handle it.

I like having Sam around.

I've never been one for kids in the past, but having him here hasn't been as horrible as I thought it would be. Like Maya said, he spends most of the time in his bedroom playing video games. If he's not in there talking to his friends—surprisingly, he doesn't yell or get upset like I've seen kids do in those viral videos—he's watching something on Netflix in the living room.

He's a good kid. Funny. A little gullible, but it's part of his charm.

We've had fun together this past week, and I'm surprised to find I'm a little sad he's leaving for his dad's right now.

Patrick is standing in the entryway, hands tucked into the pockets of his peacoat.

I'm leaning against the kitchen counter, watching him.

Maya's not here. She called me earlier to tell me Patrick wanted to make up for last weekend and pick Sam up a little early. She warned me she might not be home in time to see her son off.

She sounded both happy and sad about it.

I wanted to ask her what was up with that, but I didn't want to overstep my boundaries. Especially not after what happened the other day when I plowed right through them.

I still can't get the way she writhed on the countertop beneath me out of my head, her orgasm within reach as I lapped at her perfect fucking tits, the same counter my hands are resting on…

"This is a nice building," he says to me, pulling me from the memory that lives at the forefront of my mind. Maya and I haven't had a chance to talk about it yet, but I'm sure it's coming soon.

"Thanks."

And the silence engulfs us again.

He clears his throat a few times, and I tap my fingers against the kitchen counter.

I don't know what to say to him, and he doesn't know what to say to me.

"Sammy, you ready?" he calls out.

"Coming!"

Thank god.

The kid pads down the hall, a bag of stuff slung over his shoulder.

He's always dragging his PlayStation back and forth Maya says, and I have to say I'm a little bummed. I was looking forward to getting some practice in. The kid whoops my ass too much for my liking.

"All set?" I ask.

"Yep, except I can't find my science book. I think it's in my mom's car, but I don't have the keys. Can you tell her so she can bring it up to school tomorrow?"

"Can do, kid."

"Thanks." He holds his fist out for me to bump. "You're the best, Nolan."

"See you later, shithead."

Patrick lifts his brows at the nickname.

"Inside joke," I explain.

He nods with a grin. "I mean, you're not wrong…"

They shuffle out the door, and I let the quiet consume me.

Maya will be home any minute now, and we're going

down to River and Dean's apartment, where we'll have to pretend we didn't almost fuck in the kitchen mere days ago.

I have to wonder for the millionth time what the hell I've gotten myself into…and why it's not sending me running for the hills.

Chapter 11

MAYA

If I thought spending the last few days with Nolan was awkward after our midafternoon make-out session, it's nothing compared to being stuck inside an elevator with him as we make our way down to River and Dean's apartment.

I wanted to take the stairs, but I knew even suggesting it would have just made things worse.

The only thing we can do now is pretend nothing at all happened.

But that's hard when he's standing opposite me looking like he does.

His back is pressed against the wall, his long legs stretched out in front of him, one crossed over the other. He's wearing jeans that cling to his muscular thighs like they were tailored just for him. I've noticed he has a thing for flannel, and I don't mind it one bit because he looks damn good in the gray and black one he's currently wearing, the color making his blue eyes pop more than they already do.

He's watching me rake my gaze over him, and I can tell by the lazy smile spreading across his lips that he likes it.

I should look away, but I can't seem to force myself to do so.

Just like I can't seem to keep him off my mind.

I was so distracted at work yesterday I almost let someone walk out of the shop without charging them for half their order.

When River asked me what was wrong, I waved it off as stress.

It wasn't a complete lie. I am stressed…but not for the reasons she thinks.

Instead of worrying about all the expenses that come with a new apartment, I'm too busy preoccupied by the fact that I want to sleep with my roommate.

And I want to do it *bad*.

The elevator *finally* signals we've arrived at the right floor, and when we step out, Nolan's hand finds the small of my back as we make our way down the hall.

I swear I can feel electricity hum through me at the simple touch.

We knock on the door, and luckily we don't have to wait long before it's being swung open.

I can't help it—I burst into laughter.

Dean's grin slips right off his face and he lets out a loud sigh.

"Seriously, Maya?"

I don't answer. I'm too busy laughing.

"You, of all people? And to think you were my favorite. Looks like that's Caroline's title now."

"One I'll gladly accept!" she calls from inside the apartment.

I peek up at Nolan, and he's standing there with his mouth

hanging open.

"What?" Dean barks at him. "Got something to say?"

"Yeah, nice womb broom, you fucking hipster."

Dean reaches up and strokes the mustache that is definitely something new for him. "I'm not a hipster."

Nolan points to Dean's face. "That right there says you are."

"Dude, did you call it a womb broom?" River asks, appearing at Dean's side and shoving him out of the way. He stalks away, mumbling about his new facial hair. "This is why you're *my* favorite, Nolan."

"I resent that remark, River," Cooper complains.

She rolls her eyes. "Come on in. Just ignore Dean's face. I've learned if you don't look at it, it's like it doesn't exist."

She ushers us into the apartment, and we follow her into the kitchen.

It's weird. I've been in this same room many times over the years, but somehow, now, it feels different.

It could be because I'm with Nolan and River is with Dean and Caroline is with Cooper. It feels all...couple-y, even though Nolan and I aren't a couple.

We just can't stop making out.

"Whiskey or wine?" River holds up a bottle of each.

"Whiskey," I say, craving the burn of the alcohol to take my mind off things.

She pours me two fingers' worth of bourbon, then adds another for good measure.

Bless her.

"So, uh, what's up with the mustache?" I ask her when Dean's out of earshot.

"It's ridiculous, isn't it?" Her tone says she's annoyed, but her eyes say something entirely different. "He said he wanted to try something new. I bet he shaves it off by tomorrow night. His students are going to go nuts over it."

"It's...something."

"Does it feel good?" Caroline asks, sliding up next to us.

"You mean"—River bounces her eyebrows up and down —"good?"

Caroline and I both nod, and River bites her lip.

"Soooo good," she purrs.

I clench my thighs together, remembering how good Nolan's two-day-old scruff felt against my breasts as he lapped at them. I can only imagine how good it'd feel between my legs.

I slide my eyes his way, and I'm surprised when I find he's staring right at me, like he can read all the dirty thoughts slipping through my mind right now.

I want him.

Like, *really* want him.

These last few days have been torture trying to act like what happened between us didn't affect me, but in truth, I'm bursting at the seams to do it again.

Which is a bad idea, but I'm starting to see the appeal of Caroline's suggestion.

Our living situation is only temporary. If we go into it with clear intentions, we'll be fine. We're nothing like River and Dean, who had feelings involved before they slept together, so we're not risking anything.

We're adults, and we both clearly need the release.

We could totally make it out alive with no awkwardness. I'm certain of it.

I give my attention back to River and Caroline, who are discussing the joys of dating men who have a little scruff.

"What about you?" River asks. "Did you ever have that with Patrick?"

I want to laugh.

No, I never had that with him. Not just because he always kept his face clean-shaven, but because Patrick only went down on me once—and he didn't go anywhere near where he should have.

"Can't say I have."

"You are missing out. Better make sure the next guy you decide to bone comes with a little scruff." River bumps her shoulder into mine. "Or a womb broom."

All three of us burst into laughter, causing the guys, who are planted on the couch arguing about something, to look our way.

As if he knows what we were talking about, Nolan runs his hand over his five o'clock shadow, and I find myself squeezing my thighs together for the second time tonight.

I have no idea how I'm going to survive this evening.

"Do you want to rip his clothes off or what, Maya?" Caroline asks.

"Huh?" Heat floods my cheeks as I worry I've been caught ogling my roommate.

"Henry Cavill." She holds her phone up. "He posted this on Instagram a few minutes ago."

When River and I give her a look for knowing about it so soon, she shrugs.

"What? I have notifications turned on. Ain't no way I'm missing this."

We spend the next twenty minutes scrolling through Henry's feed, perving on his photos.

Usually, I'd be over the moon to drool over pictures of the hot-as-hell English actor.

But it's hard to get excited when the person I want most right now is sitting on the other side of the room.

At eleven thirty, we're stumbling out of River and Dean's apartment, full of food, good times, and a little too much whiskey.

Nolan presses the button for the elevator, then grins down at me. "Your best friend is a hoot."

"I could say the same thing about yours, but that mustache is…" I groan. "God, I hope he shaves it off soon."

"Hideous, isn't it?"

I nod. "I didn't want to tell River my roommate is much hotter than hers, but I think she knew."

His brows rise, and the words that just left my mouth finally hit my ears.

Luckily, he doesn't say anything as our elevator arrives. We step into the small space, and Nolan takes up the same position he did on the way down here. I mirror it.

The first floor ticks by, then the second.

The only sound is the hum of the machine working its way up the floors and the heavy breaths that seem to be caught in my chest and fighting for freedom.

We don't take our eyes off each other, and we don't speak.

Not when the elevator stops on our floor.

Not when we enter the apartment.

We don't say a word until we're standing in the hallway between our rooms, Nolan with his hand on his doorknob, me with mine on my own.

Make a move.

It's what I want to yell at him.

And what I want to keep tucked away.

"Well," he says, "thanks for a fun night."

"Yeah. It was a good time."

He exhales quietly, then pushes his door open. "Good night, Juliet."

I swallow the lump in my throat. "Night, Romeo."

I slip into my bedroom, pressing my back against the door the moment it's closed.

My heart catches in my throat, beating so loudly it's all I can hear.

I want Nolan, but I'm too scared. Too scared to mess up this good thing we have going on, too scared to do something about it.

With a heavy sigh, I push off the door and cross the room to my pile of things. I strip off my clothes and slide my oversized t-shirt on, then I crawl into my bed, pulling the covers up over my head, trying to get my heart rate to even out.

It's pointless though. I'm too keyed up. Too needy.

I need a release in a bad way.

Maybe a cold shower will help me relax.

It's late, but I'm sure Nolan won't be too annoyed if I take one. He's likely already passed out in his bed, snoring softly like he always does.

I toss my comforter off and slip out of bed, then pad to the door.

I nearly jump out of my skin when I pull it open.

Nolan's standing on the other side, hand raised and ready to knock.

The same sweats he wore the other day are slung low on his hips, and he's wearing a plain white t-shirt.

The moonlight from his bedroom window is casting a shadow across him, making him look ten times more handsome than he already is.

"Nolan? What are you—"

I don't say anything else.

I can't.

His lips are on mine, and I'm clutching him for dear life.

He slides his hands under my ass and hauls me up. I lock my legs around his waist, slipping my fingers through his hair like I've been dying to do for weeks.

I don't even realize we're moving until my back hits the wall.

I'm too focused on Nolan and what he's doing to my mouth, his hands gripping my ass tight as he rolls his hips into me.

I gasp when his dick brushes against my sensitive and much-too-neglected clit.

He chuckles against me, then reaches up, pulling my hands from his hair and pinning them against the wall above my head with one hand. He runs the fingers of his free hand up my naked thigh, and I'm so fucking excited I could burst before he even touches me.

He wrenches his mouth from mine, and I gasp for air.

"Are you drunk?" he asks, his blue eyes boring into me.

"W-What?" I stutter like a fool.

"We had a lot of whiskey downstairs—are you drunk?"

I shake my head. "Not even kind of. Are you?"

He smirks. "Only on you."

I roll my eyes and he tightens his grasp on my wrists, rolling his hips into me. He chuckles darkly when I inhale sharply at the contact.

"That's what I thought." He leans into me, running his nose along my jawline. "What would you say if I told you I can't stop thinking about you?"

"I'd say that sounds like a *you* problem."

He drives his hips into me again. Another gasp.

He laughs. "You know, I'm beginning to think you're riling me up on purpose so I'll rub my cock against that pretty pussy of yours."

Heat pools between my legs.

Nobody has said *that* word to me before...and I like it.

"You've never even seen it...how do you know it's pretty?"

He grins against me. "There's no doubt in my mind every inch of you is beautiful, Maya."

I swear my heart stops beating.

Or maybe it's because I'm holding my breath.

I exhale shakily.

"This is a bad idea, Nolan..." I remind him.

"It is."

"We're roommates."

"We are. And our best friends are dating."

"They are," I say, sucking in a sharp breath as his lips find a spot on my neck, sending a shiver down my spine. He nips at it, then rolls his tongue over it to cool the sting. "I have a kid, and you don't do relationships."

"You do, and I don't."

"So what are we going to do about that?"

He pulls his lips off me, and I already miss his touch. "What do you want to do about that?"

"I…" I lick my drying lips. "I…don't know. I like you."

"I like you too."

"And I really want to have sex with you."

He smirks. "Then what are we waiting for?"

And because we can't help it, we're kissing again, Nolan's hips driving into me in a rhythm that's going to make me come very, very soon if he doesn't stop.

Like he can sense I'm getting close, he backs off, slowing his assault.

"Just sex?" he asks against my lips.

"Just sex."

It's all he needs to hear.

He releases my tired arms and tightens his hold on me, walking us to his bedroom. His lips don't leave mine until we reach his bed, and he sets my feet on the floor. He strips his shirt off, tossing it across the room. I reach for the hem of mine, but he grabs my wrists, shaking his head.

"Not yet," he tells me.

I drop my hands to my sides, unsure what to do with them.

I let my eyes roam over his body, appreciating the way his muscles ripple under my scrutiny. There's a smattering of hair over his chest, and I itch to reach out and run my fingers through it.

Before I can, he pushes me gently until I'm seated on the edge of the bed, then he steps back, staring down at me with hungry eyes.

Unable to stop myself, I lean forward and press a kiss above the waistband of his sweats.

The touch is welcomed by his cock jumping.

"Fuck," he mutters. He bends to take my mouth in a hard kiss, sliding his fingers through my messy waves.

His touch is gentle with a hint of roughness.

I like it...*a lot.*

When he releases me, it feels like my lips are bruised, and I wonder if I'm still going to be able to feel it tomorrow.

He drops to his knees and parts mine, fitting himself between my thighs. I can feel his hot breath on my legs, and I want to slip my hands into his hair and pull him to me and put his mouth where I want it most.

I can't help the rocking of my hips.

He chuckles, enjoying the torture he's supplying right now. "What bra did you wear today?"

His question surprises me.

"Huh?"

"Was it that pink lacy one?"

"Black. It was black."

His lips curve upward in a roguish smile. "Do you want to know what I've been dying to know?"

With a gulp, I nod. I want to know anything and everything he has to tell me, especially when he's looking at me like he is.

"If your panties match your bra."

He shoulders my legs apart farther, then skates his hands up my calves and over my thighs, using one hand to push my shirt out of the way.

His eyes darken with need when he gets his answer.

"I fucking knew it."

Like he can't help himself, he leans forward, running the tip of his tongue along my slit over my black lace panties.

It's enough to make me buck against him.

His laughter vibrates against me, and I let out a whimper. I clamp my hand over my mouth, embarrassed by the desperate sounds leaving me. I've never been vocal during sex, so I'm surprised I'm making any noise at all.

He sits back on his haunches, reaching up to remove my hand.

"Don't ever be embarrassed by the sounds you make. Not with me. Got it?" I nod. "Good. Now, if you want to make good use of this hand, hold your panties while I eat your pussy."

I suck in a shocked breath.

He's serious.

He's *very* serious.

With shaky fingers, I slide my hand between my legs and pull my lace underwear to the side, exposing myself to him. I slam my eyes closed, feeling self-conscious being so bare in front of him.

"Oh, no-no," he whispers. "Open your eyes, Maya. You're going to watch me."

Is he intent on making me unable to breathe tonight?

"Open 'em," he instructs again.

I do, and he lowers his mouth to me, keeping his blue eyes trained on my gray ones the entire time.

He places gentle kisses on the sensitive areas of my inner thighs, and I was right—the feel of his five o'clock shadow is exhilarating as he presses kisses everywhere except where I want him most.

"Nolan." His name comes out a growl, and his shoulders shake.

"Something the matter, Maya?"

151

"You know exactly what's the—"

He flattens his tongue against my clit, and my eyes flutter closed at the connection.

He pulls away, and I know what I did wrong before he even says a word.

I peel my eyes open to see a satisfied smirk on his lips.

"Quick learner, I see."

I push my feet onto my toes and spread my legs farther apart. He buries his face between them at the invitation, his hands kneading my thighs as he gets lost in me and I get lost in him.

This time when he fits his tongue against my clit, I don't dare close my eyes, too scared he's going to stop.

And holy shit I don't want him to stop.

He works me over with his tongue, switching between long, languid strokes and sucking my sensitive bud into his mouth. I'm squirming against him, practically fucking his face, and he's loving every minute of it. *I'm* loving every minute of it. Especially when he shoves his sweats down and frees his long cock, fisting it as he drags me closer and closer to the edge of bliss.

The sight alone is almost enough to make me come.

"Please," I whimper. "I need to…"

He relents in his teasing, giving me what I need. He sucks my bud into his mouth again, this time with more pressure, and I explode against him.

Unable to hold myself up anymore, I collapse against the bed as he laps at me, pulling me down from the high.

I miss his touch the moment he pulls away, but he's right back over me, pulling me up into a sitting position, sliding my shirt over my head.

His fingers graze over my nipples and the sensation goes straight to my core.

I'm already ready for him again.

His lips find the spot right above my collarbone that he somehow already knows drives me wild, and he kisses me like he owns me, nipping at my lips, then trailing his mouth up to my ear.

"Middle of the bed, Maya." His tongue flits out and he traces the shell of my ear. "Hands and knees."

I don't dare argue.

I do as he says, crawling to the center of the mattress and getting into the position requested.

I'm giddy with anticipation as I hear him push his sweats down his legs, then riffle around in the medicine cabinet in his bathroom.

Finally, the corner of the bed dips as he crawls onto it behind me, his heat enveloping me as he settles himself.

His cock brushes against my ass and my hips move of their own accord, seeking his touch.

He laughs, palming my ass cheeks, kneading them. "Someone's needy."

"It's been a while."

"How long?"

"Too fucking long, and all this talking is making the time even longer. I'm—" His cockhead presses against my opening, and I hiss at the contact. "*Yesssss.* Please."

"Are you sure?"

I push my hips back in response.

He sinks into me, not stopping until he's fully seated.

"Fuck." He draws the word out in a deep growl, dropping his head between my shoulders. "So fucking good."

I want to cry. Scream.

It's been so long since I've felt so full, and I don't think there's ever been a time it's felt this good.

"Tell me I can move, Maya." I can feel the sweat beading up on his forehead as he holds himself back. "I *need* to move."

"Move."

"Thank fuck."

The words are barely out of his mouth before he's slamming into me. *Hard.*

It hurts and feels like heaven at the same time.

Nolan fits me like a puzzle piece I didn't know I was missing.

His hands dig into my hips, and I know I'm going to have a bruise tomorrow. It will be absolutely worth it.

I reach between my legs, rubbing my clit in small circles as he buries himself inside me over and over, hitting the deep spot that makes me see stars.

My orgasm races through me, catching me off guard, and I collapse into the bed with exhaustion.

Nolan doesn't stop, his hips bucking against me faster…*harder.*

And then he follows me over the edge.

He falls against me, his forehead dropping back between my shoulders, lips brushing against my skin gently, a stark contrast to what he just did to me.

"You've ruined me, Juliet," he whispers against my skin.

I smile, wanting to tell him he's ruined me too, but sleep claims me before I can.

Chapter 12

NOLAN

I'm burning alive.

Or at least that's what it feels like to have Maya spread out over me. Her leg is slung over mine, her head resting on my chest as she snores quietly, a pool of drool forming on my chest. She runs hot, and the mass of hair she has doesn't help any. My arm is asleep and I've been uncomfortable for the last hour, but I wouldn't trade a second of this for anything.

Rain beats against the window. There's no way I'll be going in to work today. I've never been more grateful for a day off before because the last thing I want to do is get out of this bed right now.

"Butter," she mutters, and I laugh.

It's the fourth time she's said something nonsensical like that.

Who knew Maya talks in her sleep?

She sounds like she's making a grocery list because the first thing she said was *noodles*, followed by *beans* and *rice*.

She huffs out a breath, her hair blowing up and flitting across my nose. It tickles, causing me to twitch under her.

She stirs, and I still, scared I've woken her up.

She peels her eyes open just the slightest bit, then they flutter closed again.

But I feel it.

Her heart rate changes, and suddenly she's shoving away from me, pushing on my chest so hard I grunt as she scrambles away. Her eyes are wide and wild as she takes in the room around her, like she's not sure where she is.

Finally, her stare lands on me, then it slides down my naked body that's covered by nothing but a sheet…the same one pooled around her waist, exposing those perfect tits I'm dying to get another taste of.

I quirk up a brow. "Morning."

"It wasn't a dream?"

I smirk, unsure how I feel about the question considering all the things I just heard her say. "No, it wasn't."

A blush steals up her cheeks. "Oh."

It's a good oh, that much I can tell.

What worries me are all the other emotions flitting through her peculiar gray eyes.

Confusion.

Panic.

Regret.

"I have to pee."

Without another word, she hops off the bed and races to the bathroom, locking herself inside.

All right then.

I push myself up until I'm sitting against my headboard and blow out a breath.

I still can't wrap my mind around last night. One minute I

was telling her good night, the next I was about to knock on her door, ready to beg her to let me touch her again.

I *had* to touch her again. There was no doubt about it.

We'd spent the night downstairs at River and Dean's having fun with our friends and drinking too much and trying way too fucking hard to ignore the tension brewing between us.

I can't count the number of times I caught her peeking my way with yearning in her eyes. She wanted me as badly as I wanted her, and since we've been playing a dangerous game since she moved in, I wasn't surprised when she was as ready to call a truce as I was.

Last night was…*wow*.

It was easily the best sex I've had of my life. I can't remember a time I've come so hard. I didn't even make it to the bathroom to pull the condom off. I tossed it into a tissue and fell asleep the moment I wrapped my arms around Maya's warm body.

She was so responsive to my touch. So trusting. So damn beautiful.

I want to do it again. *Badly*.

And soon.

The bathroom door is pulled open, and a very naked Maya waltzes back into the room.

I like how confident she is in front of me, not trying to hide herself like most would.

She slips back under the covers, sliding up next to me. She doesn't say anything, just sets her head on my shoulder.

I can't stop myself from pressing a kiss to her forehead.

"That was…*wow*."

I chuckle. "A good wow?"

"No. Totally bad. I thought for sure your dick would be bigger."

I snort, peering down at her. "That so?"

She nods, her lips setting into a grim line. "By at least a few inches. What a disappointment…"

"It's weird…I didn't hear you complaining last night. In fact, I'm pretty sure you were begging for me."

"I was? Huh. You must have misheard me because—"

She shrieks when I slide an arm around her and swing her over my lap until she's straddling me.

My already hard cock rubs against her clit, eliciting a moan from her still swollen lips.

"Don't think I misheard that."

I thrust against her again and swallow her next moan with my mouth. Her tongue slips in against mine and her hands curl into my hair, tugging me closer as she rubs her pussy against me, needing the friction as much as I do.

"Nolan…" My name falls from her lips on a plea and I palm her ass, dragging her over my leaking cock.

"I need a condom," I tell her.

She pulls back. "I'm on the pill and I never miss one."

"Are you sure? I've never not used one and got tested at my doctor's appointment."

She nibbles at her bottom lip as she continues to rub against me like she can't help it. She brushes her nose against mine, pressing our foreheads together.

"I'm sure, Nolan," she whispers. "I trust you. Make me feel good."

She doesn't have to ask me twice.

I dig my fingers into her hips, and using my shoulders for leverage, she rises up enough for me to slip inside her.

"Oh, fuck," I groan, tossing my head back as I slide in until I can't anymore.

She lets out a low moan, her pussy gripping me tight. She feels as good as she did last night.

No.

Better.

I knew being with Maya would be good, but I didn't realize how good. I could live inside of her and never get tired of it.

I capture a nipple with my lips, sucking it while she rides me lazily, the exact opposite of how I fucked her last night.

Her pants grow louder, and I know she's getting close.

I reach between us, finding her clit and pressing my thumb against it, rubbing circles.

It's enough to send her over the edge and she tosses her head back, constricting around me, her pussy milking me, begging me to follow behind her. I thrust into her a few more times and my orgasm races through me so fast I barely pull out in time before I spill my load onto her stomach.

"Holy shit," she mutters, dropping her head against my shoulder, satisfied and worn out. "So good."

Too fucking good.

"I'm so happy this place serves breakfast all day." Maya takes a long drag from her steaming mug, scanning the restaurant. "Some days I swear I could live off breakfast food alone."

We spent all morning in bed, not leaving until both our stomachs were louder than our moans. We've yet to figure out a grocery schedule, so when we finally ventured out to the kitchen, the fridge was bare.

The Gravy Train sounded like the next best thing to spreading Maya out on the counter and having my own feast.

I scrub a hand over the scruff lining my jaw. I could use a shave, but hearing Maya's reaction to the feel of it between her legs this morning…well, maybe I'll keep it for now.

"I can get on board with that. I'd eat pancakes just about every day of the week if I thought I could get away with it."

She wrinkles her nose. "Nah. But I wouldn't kick a plate of eggs, bacon, and potatoes out of the daily rotation."

"Those are good options too, but let's be honest, the best breakfast of all time is—"

"Biscuits and gravy," she finishes for me. "I know River and Dean are all about the pie, but give me some good sausage gravy and homemade biscuits any day."

"If I wasn't already sleeping with you, that would have sealed the deal right there."

"That's all it would have taken?"

There's a twinkle in her eye that wasn't there before, and I'm about ninety-nine percent sure it has to do with all the orgasms I've given her.

She looks tired, but in that good kind of way. Her lips are still swollen from my kisses, and there's a red spot above her collarbone where I might have spent too much time.

She's gorgeous, and I already can't wait to get back in my bed.

"Way to a man's heart is through his stomach." I wink.

Something flits across her eyes, a crinkle forming between her brows for the briefest of seconds.

Before I can ask what's wrong, Darlene drops off our

meals—biscuits and gravy for us both—and refills our mugs. She promises to be back to check on us soon and scurries off.

We tuck into our breakfast, too busy filling our far-too-empty stomachs to make conversation.

Maya doesn't speak again until we're both scraping the bottom of our plates.

"Should we talk about what happened?"

I push my empty plate away and lean back against the booth, stuffed to the gills with carbs. "I thought we discussed it plenty last night."

She purses her lips, tipping her head to the side, studying me. "Just sex, right?"

"Just sex," I agree.

Her lips pull into a smile, but it doesn't reach her eyes. "Good. Glad we're on the same page."

We absolutely are.

Just sex. It means nothing else at all.

She's not staying, and even if she were, it wouldn't matter. A relationship with a single mom is the last thing I want to get wrapped up in. I don't do love, and I certainly don't do kids.

We're just having fun until she moves out, and then we'll move on like adults.

No harm, no foul...right?

Maya: I know you hate texting, but I had to tell you this now...

Maya: When I first moved in, I promised I'd cook you a warm meal every night, but I'm tired because someone

kept me up past my bedtime last night and I've been dealing with old, cranky ladies all day.

Me: That's a long-winded way to ask if I'm okay with takeout for dinner.

Maya: I'm so glad you could read between the lines.

Maya: Is that okay? I'm sorry for not cooking.

Me: I'm going to pretend you didn't just say that.

Me: Takeout is fine. Anything particular in mind?

Maya: Pizza doesn't sound bad unless you'd rather have something else.

Me: I never say no to pizza. I'm pretty sure that's a sin or something.

Maya: Good. I'll grab a large cheese on the way home.

Me: Cheese? Is this even really Maya?

Maya: I figured I'd save some cash on the toppings since I expect you're bringing the meats. ;-)

I shift, and damn am I glad as hell I'm wearing pants that'll easily conceal the bulge in my pants if someone were to look over here.

We've fallen into a pattern over the past several days. I come home, we have dinner together, and then we crawl into my bed to explore what makes us tick until neither of us can move.

Maya's appetite for sex is insatiable to the point I worry *I* won't be able to keep up with *her*.

Part of me wonders if she's making up for all the shitty sex she's had before. Or maybe she's getting her fill until this inevitably ends, which is exactly what I'm doing.

Me: As long as you bring dessert…

Maya: I know I started it, but we have to stop. I'm getting turned on at work.

Me: Tease.

Maya: Funny coming from you.

Maya: See you at home, Romeo.

"Who are you texting?"

"Huh?" I peel my eyes off my screen.

Jake nods toward my phone. "You've been grinning like a fool for the last five minutes. You haven't even finished your turkey sandwich yet, so I assume it's a girl." His lips curl in disgust as he glances down at his own meal. "Which I'm jealous of. My wife packed me peanut butter and jelly again."

His disgust takes me back to a time when Dean used to trade his meaty sandwiches for mine because all my dad could afford was peanut butter. I couldn't stomach it for the longest time.

But I'd take that bullet for Jake if it means it'll distract him from asking too many questions about who I'm texting.

"Wanna trade?"

"No way." He holds the sandwich to his chest. "She cut the crusts off, man." He nods toward my phone again. "You'll understand when your girl starts packing your lunch."

"I don't have a girl."

He snorts. "Sure you don't."

"I don't," I insist, puffing my chest out.

"A guy doesn't stare at his phone grinning like an idiot if he didn't have a girl he's talking to on the other end." He sends me a pointed glance. "Who is she?"

"She's no one."

He grins. "So it *is* a girl." His eyes widen. "Oh fuck, is it the hot chick from the diner? The one who's living with you now?"

"She was texting me about dinner." *And sex.* "But she's not my girl. Just my roommate."

"You're telling me you haven't slept with her yet?"

"I haven't slept with her."

"Wow, man." He shakes his head. "That's how you're gonna do me?"

I pinch my brows together. "What do you mean?"

"We've worked side by side for the last five years, Brooks —I can tell when you're blowing smoke up my ass."

Fuck.

"All right, fine. We slept together. Big deal."

"Big deal is damn right. She's your roommate. That's nothing to turn your nose up at."

"It's not permanent."

"Her living there or you two fucking?"

"Both."

He huffs out a laugh. "Right. Keep selling that shit to yourself." He crams the rest of his sandwich in his mouth, then hops off the tailgate. "I'll see you in there."

I'm not selling myself anything. We both agreed it was just sex, and I mean it on my end. I've had friends with benefits before and walked away unscathed.

This is no different.

I'm sure of it.

Chapter 13

MAYA

Time is passing faster than I thought it ever could.

This last week and a half I've spent with Nolan has been nothing short of magical.

The things he's done to me…

The stuff I've done to him…

I swear I've been flying above the clouds for days now.

I'm starting to wonder if I'll ever get tired of him, but every day I wake up next to him, it makes me want him more.

We've been discreet since Sam came home from his dad's. I set an alarm every night in case I fall asleep, then sneak back over to my room before the sun—and my kid—rises.

"Good morning," I tell him as he pads out of his bedroom in his work pants and unbuttoned flannel that shows off a white shirt clinging to the muscles I've raked my fingers over so many times I've lost count. I set a fresh plate of pancakes on the counter, knowing he loves them. "You're just in time."

"What's all this for?" he asks, dropping down onto a stool.

"I wanted pancakes," Sam says through a full mouth.

Nolan's eyes find mine. *Is that why you left so early?* they ask.

Yes, mine answer.

"Well, good call, Sam. I love pancakes."

"That's what Mom said too." He shovels another forkful of fluffy goodness into his gob. "And you're lucky she makes the best ones ever."

"I'll be the judge of that."

He slathers butter on the perfectly round and golden cakes, then pours a generous amount of syrup on them and takes a bite.

I feel I've recently become an expert on what Nolan finds pleasurable, and I can tell right away he loves my pancakes.

"Well?" Sam asks, watching him closely.

"Not bad."

"Not bad?! They're way better than the place my dad takes me, and that's at, like, a restaurant. That's gotta mean something."

"Not true. Restaurants can suck at cooking too."

"Yeah, like the diner my dad always goes to. Their food is so...*blech*." He sticks his tongue out, shaking his head. "Dad has awful taste."

"Hey! That is a direct insult to me, the woman he used to date."

He shrugs. "I'm just stating facts, Mom."

"Nolan's right. You are a shithead." I toss a hand towel at him.

"Hey! Not in the pancakes, lady!"

"Don't call me lady. And go finish getting ready for school."

"Do I have to go?"

"Yes. It's illegal if you don't, and I really don't feel like going to jail."

"Why can't you live a little and break the law, Mom?"

"Yeah, *Mom*," Nolan teases. "Live a little, huh?"

I point a finger at him. "I'll send your ass to school right along with him." I look at Sam. "Go brush your teeth."

With a sigh, he pushes his empty plate across the counter. "Fine—but only because I'm looking forward to chicken nugget day at lunch."

I shake my head as he slinks out of the kitchen. "Remind me again why I had a kid?"

"Because the condom broke?"

I laugh. "Fuck condoms."

"I agree." Heat blazes in his eyes, and I bet he's thinking about the same thing I am.

How just an hour ago I was snuggled in his bed after a long night of us trying our hardest to be quiet during sex where we definitely *did not* use a condom.

"Speaking of…" He leans across the counter and I match his movements, dragging my tongue along my bottom lip as he stares at me like he wants to kiss me senseless.

"Hey, Nolan?" Sam says, shuffling down the hall.

We jump apart like we've been doing something we shouldn't be.

And really, we shouldn't be.

We've done a good job of keeping this hidden from Sam, and we need to continue doing so. He doesn't need to see us together, thinking this is something it's not—something permanent.

"I was wondering," he continues, popping around the corner, "I'm having a talent show at school in a couple of weeks. Dean's teaching me how to play the guitar. You're coming, right?"

"Talent show, huh?" He runs his hand over his chin, pretending to think. I've noticed he's been keeping the growth on his face for a few days before shaving it off, and I suspect it has everything to do with me and how much I like it. "Depends on what song Dean is teaching you. He has awful taste in music."

"He keeps trying to make me sing Bob Slinger songs, and I hate them."

I tuck my lips together, trying not to laugh. "Bob Seger, not Slinger."

"Whatever." He shrugs. "I just know I don't like it. Can you teach me a different song?"

"Well, I don't know how to play guitar, except for on the PlayStation, but tell Dean to teach you a song by Foo Fighters or I'm going to tell River about that thing he doesn't want me to tell her."

"What's a food fighter?"

"Kid, you are killing me right now." Nolan clutches his chest. "Not food, *Foo* Fighters. Just tell Dean what I said."

Sam's eyes brighten. "You think that will work?"

"Oh yeah." Nolan pushes off his stool, making his way around the counter into the kitchen, then deposits his empty plate onto the countertop. "I know it will."

"Cool. Mario Kart race tonight after practice?"

Before we moved in, I worried most about Nolan and Sam getting along, especially knowing how Nolan feels about kids, but I don't understand why he says he doesn't like them. He gets along with Sam just fine, and they're always off playing video games together or watching true crime documentaries—

something I'm not super keen on, but until Sam gets freaked out, it's fine. Any time we go out to the grocery store or the diner and he sees a kid, Nolan's always making faces at them and making them laugh.

Sometimes I think he's better with them than I am, and I'm the parent.

"It's on, but only if I get to be Mario."

"Mario is lame. Dibs on Bowser!"

"Dibs on getting you to school on time!" I hate interrupting their moment, but if I don't get Sam out of this apartment in the next five minutes, he'll be late. "Do you have your homework?"

Sam snaps his fingers. "That's what I was forgetting. Be right back."

Nolan grins after him. "Man, that kid is exhausting."

"But lovable." I lean back against the counter. "So, what's the thing Dean doesn't want River to know?"

"Nuh-huh," he says, running his plate under the faucet, then putting it into the dishwasher. He dries his hands on a towel and faces me. "I'm not telling you. You'll run right to her and I won't be able to hold it over Dean's head."

"I would not run right to her!"

"Please. She's your best friend. You tell her everything."

Not everything.

I still haven't told her I'm sleeping with Nolan, and I'm not sure what's stopping me.

Maybe because telling someone would make it more real?

Maybe because getting more people involved would make it harder to walk away from?

"That's not true. I have...secrets." His eyes widen at that

169

confession. "What? Because I'm a woman I'm incapable of keeping my mouth shut?"

"I didn't say that. I'm just curious what you're hiding from her."

Us.

I shrug. "Stuff."

"Is it"—he shifts a finger between the two of us—"this?"

"That's one of the things."

"Ashamed?" I give him an *Are you serious?* look. "Because you didn't sound ashamed last night when I was eat—"

I clamp my hand over his mouth. "Stop it!" I hiss.

He laughs against me, then pulls my hand from his mouth, holding my palm open.

"I'm just saying—you better not be ashamed of us. I'd be offended."

He presses a kiss to my palm. It's light and sweet, very different from how he kisses me at night, and my breath gets caught in my throat for a moment.

He closes my fingers around it. "Keep that for later."

His words feel intimate, wrapping around me like silk, and my hands tremble.

I don't understand what's happening, but it's not something that's ever happened before...and I don't know if I like it.

He drops my hand, stepping away from me just before Sam comes around the corner.

I swallow the knot forming in my throat, looking anywhere but at Nolan.

"All right," Sam says, his shoulders sinking. "Let's get this day over with."

"Are you telling me you don't eat cornbread with chili?"

"Uh, no. I wasn't aware I was supposed to." Nolan's eyes flit down the aisle. "Don't go too far, Sam," he calls to my son before looking back down at me like he didn't just pull a dad move. "We've always had peanut butter sandwiches with it."

"What?" I curl my lip in disgust. "You can't be serious."

"I am, but we also ate a lot of peanut butter in my house. They always had it at the food pantry, so we'd find anything we could eat it with. I've never had chili any other way."

My heart squeezes at his words.

Given how much my life has changed in the last few years, sometimes I forget Nolan and I grew up in different worlds. Up until I was sixteen, I lived in a gorgeous house with my parents who had been married since what seemed like the dawn of time. I was a good kid who got good grades. We attended church every Sunday, and we took brownies to our neighbors on the regular. I didn't want for anything and was even a little spoiled.

He doesn't talk about his dad a lot, but from what he has mentioned, it's clear they had a rough time.

"How about we try both? Sam can test each option, and he'll be the tiebreaker."

"I'm not sure I trust his judgment because you've been poisoning his mind for the last twelve years, but"—he sticks his hand out—"you're on."

I slide my palm against his and he yanks me into him.

We're so close I can feel his lips ghost against my ear as he whispers, "But just so you know, if he cheats, you'll be the one getting punished for it later."

His words are full of sexual promises, and I'm pretty sure I'll be getting "punished" no matter what.

He steps away from me like he didn't just cause my panties to soak in the middle of the grocery store.

It's not the first time he's done it this trip either. It's like he enjoys seeing me squirm in public.

Or in general.

Like the other night when we were finishing up some documentary with Sam. The moment my son got up to go to the bathroom, Nolan hauled me into him and kissed me until I couldn't breathe.

Sam asked why I was out of breath when he came back.

"Well, well, well. What do we have here? Don't you two look domestic as fuck."

I whirl around to see Dean standing at the end of the aisle, eyes flitting back and forth between me and his best friend, who is halfway down the aisle with Sam.

Oh shit. Did he see us? Did he hear *us?*

"Dean!" His name comes out a squeak, and we all hear how off it sounds. "What are you doing here?"

He holds up a box of tampons. "Your best friend sent me for Satan's cotton fingers."

"And I'm sure she loves you putting it on blast for everyone to see." I smack the box down. "You're supposed to be discreet with those."

"Why? She's not discreet about it. She screamed to the entire diner this morning about her cramps when they ran out of cherry pie."

"Did they run out of pie or did you race her down the sidewalk again and get the last piece?"

A pink blush steals up his cheeks and he shrugs. "She should really work on her pace."

I can't help but laugh. "You're a terrible boyfriend."

He holds the tampons up again. "This says otherwise."

"Dude, you finally shaved off the womb broom!" Nolan's brows crease as he approaches us. "Why are you holding lady corks?"

"Oh my god. Does every single member of the male population have a slang word for tampons?"

They look at me like I'm dumb, nodding.

"Of course we do," Dean says. "If we have to hear about this shit, we're going to at least make it fun for us."

"Yes, because a woman on her menstrual cycle is all about what makes *you* comfortable."

"Ew," Sam says, walking up to us. "We had to learn about that in class. Hi, Dean."

"'Sup, Sammy?" They bump their fists together.

"Don't say ew," Nolan tells him. "It's a natural thing. Totally normal and not disgusting. Got it?" Sam nods. "Good. Did you get the chips?"

I stare up at Nolan, impressed by him yet again for the way he is with Sam.

Sam holds up a bag of plain chips. "These okay?"

"Can you grab a bag of flavored ones too?"

"On it!"

"And some Fritos!" I call after him. Then I twist back around to Dean. "You better get some for River too. She loves Fritos on her period."

"You just saved my life, likely literally."

"Even though I'm sure you don't deserve it, you're welcome."

He doesn't take offense, probably because I'm right.

"So, what are you two up to tomorrow night? I'm sure River would love for you guys to come down and hang again."

Memories of the last time we went to River and Dean's flood me.

"Can't."

"We can't?" I ask, surprised by Nolan's answer.

"We're going furniture shopping tomorrow after you drop Sam off, remember?"

We didn't make plans to go shopping, but I can read loud and clear what his eyes are saying.

I have plans to make you scream.

"Oh, yeah. I remember," I lie. "Nolan wants to get a kitchen table and a couch for when I finally get my life together and move out."

Nolan's eyes darken for only a moment before he pastes on a smile that doesn't reach his eyes. "Figured I'd get started shopping now in case I have to order something and wait on it."

"It's about time you officially move into your place," Dean says, clapping him on the back. "Proud of you. Growing up so fast."

Nolan shrugs his hand off, scowling at him. "Shut the fuck up and get those spirit sticks to your girlfriend before she really does kill you and I have to help her bury the body."

"Aw. You'd do that for her?"

"I'm pretty sure you're not supposed to say *aw* about your own murder," I point out.

"Nah. Just means my boy here loves my girl." He pats

Nolan's chest. "Holy shit—that means there *is* a heart in there. I knew it!"

"Dean..." Nolan growls.

"All right, all right. I'm leaving. Try to keep your hands to yourselves, you crazy kids."

He winks at us, and it sends my heart into overdrive as he waltzes away whistling.

I whirl on Nolan as soon as he's gone.

"What did that mean? Do you think he saw us?"

"I don't know." Nolan shrugs. "Who the hell knows what Dean is saying half the time."

"He was standing there when you..." I trail off, knowing he's aware of what I'm referring to.

"Even if he did see something, he won't say anything."

I chew on my bottom lip, not so sure.

Nolan reaches over, using his thumb to pluck my lip from between my teeth. "Stop that. I don't want them all chewed on when I'm kissing them later." I grin at that. "Don't worry about it, okay?"

I nod. "Okay."

My head gets the memo, but my heart doesn't.

Chapter 14

NOLAN

We haven't come up for air all week long.

With Sam at his dad's, Maya hasn't had to sneak out of my bedroom in the wee hours of the morning, and I can't say I'm sad about it.

I've never been so excited to wake up with her lying next to me.

I'm trying really fucking hard to not think about that fact too much.

"You know," she says, head on my chest as she runs her fingers through the hair there, "we should probably actually go furniture shopping at some point so you have something when I move out. I don't want to leave you empty-handed when I take my couch back, and you really should get a kitchen table for whenever you have guests over."

I don't ever have guests over.

Hell, other than Dean (and River because they're attached at the fucking hip), I haven't had another person in my apartment in the few months I've lived here. I never had anyone over when I lived at my old place, and not because it was too small.

Inviting someone into your living space is intimate. It's showing them a side of you that's literally locked behind a closed door.

If she's hinting at me bringing women back here after we're done doing whatever this is, she's way off the mark.

Instead, I say, "I think that's a good idea."

"Do you want to go now?"

No.

Honestly, I just want to stay in bed with her all day.

Sam comes home from his dad's tomorrow, and we'll have to go back to being careful.

I like not being careful and want to take advantage of it.

"We can grab lunch on our way there. I think I could use some fuel anyway."

Food does sound good. "I'm down."

Neither of us moves to get up, and we laugh at our laziness.

Finally, Maya pushes off my chest, sitting up to stare down at me. The blanket pools around her hips, baring her tits to me.

Unable to stop myself, I reach up, pulling an already beaded nipple into my mouth.

She groans, her hand finding my head. She runs her fingers through my hair, pulling me closer as I flatten my tongue over her. Her grip tightens, and I know it's getting to her like we didn't just fuck.

She tugs at my hair. "We should take a break."

I peer up at her. "Is that what you really want?"

"No, but I am starving."

Her stomach gurgles, and I chuckle, relenting. "All right, I see your point. We'll recharge and reconvene later."

"You go shower first, then I'll take one. I can just let my hair air dry."

"Or—and hear me out—we shower together."

Her lips form an O, surprised by my suggestion.

For some reason unknown to me, despite seeing every inch of one another over the last few weeks, we've not once showered together. Even though I've never showered with someone else before, it seems silly to continue to keep taking separate ones.

"Unless you're not comfortable with that…"

Her eyes drop to the bed and she picks at an invisible fuzzy. "It's just…my ex was always weird about it. I used to sneak in there with him, trying to be the sexy, spontaneous wife, until one day he exploded on me about invading his space. I never did it again." She shrugs. "It's dumb, I know. But I was young, and it really stung. It's stuck with me since."

I like Patrick just fine, but moments like this, seeing the usually confident Maya so damn defeated…I want to smack the asshole upside the head.

I hook my finger under her chin, bringing her eyes up to mine.

"Well, and I mean this with all the offense in the world, he's a fucking moron." She laughs. "And he clearly has no idea how much fun can be had in the shower."

Her brows shoot up. "Oh, so *that's* why you want to shower together."

"Well, duh. What'd you think I was going to do, wash your hair or something?"

"Oh, man. I love getting my hair washed. I swear sometimes that's the only reason I get my hair cut at all."

"That shit does feel really good."

"So good." That doubt creeps back into her eyes. "Are you sure you want to? I really don't mind taking one after you..."

I sigh. "I'm sure, Maya. It really fucks me up though that he made you feel like you weren't worth his time. That makes me real pissed off at him."

"Don't be," she says. "He wasn't an awful husband."

I scoff. "He sure as shit sounds like it. I got a glimpse of how a man should love a woman, and that's not the way you do it at all."

She tips her head, so many questions swirling in her eyes.

I don't usually talk about my mom leaving, but something has me wanting to spill all my secrets to her.

"My mom bailed the year I turned five. Told my dad she'd fallen in love with someone else, packed her shit, and left. My dad...he was devastated."

A light bulb goes off for her. "Ah. Hence your hesitation with relationships."

I nod, pushing past the lump in my throat. "Even though she left him high and dry, up until he died, he was still madly in love with her. *That's* how you love a woman."

Tears well in her eyes, and I hope she doesn't start crying because I don't know what I'd do if she did.

She blinks them back, then huffs out a breath. "I'm sorry, Nolan."

I shrug. "Is what it is."

"Yeah, but—"

I silence her, pressing my lips to hers, and she melts into my touch as I kiss her senseless.

"Don't think I don't know what you're up to…" she says, coming up for air, rubbing her nose against mine.

"I don't want to talk about that shit. I have better things in mind." Pulling away, I throw the blanket off and slip out of the bed. I hold my hand out to her. "Come on. Let's get wet and wild."

She smirks. "You're really lame sometimes, you know that?"

"All part of my charm, baby."

She screws her face up, sliding her hand into mine and letting me haul her up. "No. I don't like that one."

"Huh?"

"The endearment. I like Juliet better."

"Duly noted." I smack her ass. "Now get in there and start the water. I'll be right there."

She sashays into the bathroom, and I hear the water hit the shower floor.

By the time I join her, she's already under the stream of hot water. I've never been jealous of water before, but watching it roll over her skin…I am.

"Is that my shampoo?" She nods toward the bottle in my hand as I step into the shower.

"Yep. Now scoot over and stop hogging all the hot water."

She rolls her eyes and moves over no more than an inch, her back to me. Tipping her head back, she lets the water wash over her as I flip open the bottle of shampoo and squirt a healthy amount onto my hands.

She jumps when my fingers find her head, then relaxes

into my touch as I lather up the shampoo, letting a few soft moans escape her lips.

I wash her hair once, then again for good measure, and I know she's loving every second of it.

Just like I know there's no way she misses my cock brushing against her ass.

When all the shampoo is rinsed out, she turns, and there's something in her gaze that has my chest feeling funny.

I don't know what it means, but I know I don't completely hate it.

And that makes me uneasy.

Instead of dwelling on it, I crush my lips to hers.

She wraps her legs around me. I press her back against the wall and slide into her.

And I fuck her until I don't feel it anymore.

"So, what do you think?" The saleswoman clasps her hands, smiling down at us with that customer service smile all salespeople have. "Is this the one?"

"Hmmm…" Maya says, tapping her finger against her chin. "Can we have a few moments to discuss it?"

"Of course!" the woman says cheerfully. She points to a desk in the center of the room. "I'll be right over there. Give me a wave whenever you're ready to get this baby loaded up in your truck." She gives us another megawatt grin, then shuffles away, leaving us in our blissful state.

We've been sitting on this couch for the last fifteen minutes, letting our bodies sink into the cushions.

I decided the moment we sat down this was the winner,

but Maya insisted we needed to sit on each couch for at least fifteen minutes before we made a final decision.

"Are you sure this is the one you want?" she asks once we're alone. "The thing is massive and will take up your whole living room."

"So? Isn't the point of the living room to live in it? If I buy this thing, I'll definitely be living in there. Do you like it?"

"It doesn't matter what I like. It's not my couch."

"Then why are you trying to talk me out of it?"

"I'm not. I'm just playing devil's advocate."

"I'm pretty sure the devil doesn't need more of those."

She shrugs. "Just doing my duty as your official decorator."

"Tell me, official decorator, other than it being too big—though that's not an attribute you've been complaining about lately—does this couch have any qualities you're not fond of?"

She bounces up and down a few times, patting the cushions. "No. It's a solid couch. Sturdy. It'll hold up for all those extracurricular activities you're so fond of."

"I'm going to assume you're not referring to my Netflix marathons."

She gives me a flirty grin, her eyes sparkling with mischief. "I was thinking more horizontally."

"Oh. Like this?"

I pounce on her and she shrieks as I pin her to the couch, her hands above her head. I'm glad we're at the back of the building, tucked away in our own little corner so no one can see us.

"Nolan!" She wiggles under me in an attempt to escape—

a big mistake because I can already feel my cock stirring to life—as I pepper kisses across her face. "Stop it! I was teasing!"

"You were not. You like my horizontal marathons on the couch."

"I do. Which reminds me...maybe I should be couch shopping too. We've spent far too much time on it for it to be sanitary any longer."

She's not wrong there. If we're not in my bed, we're on the couch...or on the kitchen counter...or on the living room floor.

With the addition of my shower just hours ago, I've had her almost all over the apartment at this point.

All but her bedroom.

And man do I want to take her in the library so badly.

I hit the spot above her collarbone and she moans, arching into my touch as I tease the skin between her jeans and t-shirt where it has ridden up.

"Nolan..." She sighs.

A throat is cleared, and we both freeze.

We peek up at the intruder, and the last person I'm expecting to see is standing over us.

"C-Caroline," Maya says, shoving at my chest. I take the hint and roll off her, spreading my legs to help alleviate the pressure in my throbbing dick. "Cooper." She clears her throat. "Uh, what are you guys doing here?"

They smirk down at us like they caught us with our hands in the cookie jar.

And I guess they kind of did.

Cooper hitches his thumb Caroline's way. "Caroline broke my office chair trying to give me a lap dance."

"Cooper!" Her cheeks turn a bright red. "What the hell!"

"What?" He lifts his shoulders. "It's true. You have awful coordination. I mean, that's what got us into this mess in the first place—when you tripped in the hallway and grabbed my junk."

"This mess? You mean our *relationship*?"

He shrugs again, and Caroline rolls her eyes. Cooper's darken at her reaction, and I bet she'll be catching hell for it later.

"I'd ask what you guys are doing, but that's kind of obvious." Caroline giggles. "Glad to see you took my suggestion, Maya."

"What suggestion?" I ask Maya.

"Nothing," she mumbles. "It's nothing."

It doesn't sound like nothing, but I drop it because Maya looks mortified right now.

She hasn't told River about us, just like I haven't told Dean.

And now that Caroline knows…it means they will soon too.

Which is fine. I don't care what they have to say about it. We're adults and we know what we're doing.

Maya shoots up from the couch, grabbing Caroline's arm and dragging her away, leaving me alone with Cooper as they put their heads together, whispering.

"So…this happened."

I laugh, shoving up off the couch. "It did."

"Does Dean know?"

I shake my head. "No, and I'd rather he not find out."

"Understood." He nods, glancing back at the girls. "Is it serious?"

"Come on, man. You know I don't do relationships. We're just having some fun."

He furrows his brows together, eyeing me with a sharp gaze that has me shifting from one foot to the other.

"What?" I snap, unable to take it any longer.

"Nothing, man. Just...I hope you know what you're doing."

"I do."

But, fuck, my words are lacking conviction even to my own ears.

I ignore it.

"I appreciate the concern," I tell him, "but we got this."

His eyes tell me he doesn't believe me, but he nods anyway. "All right."

The girls make their way back over, and the tension between the four of us is thick.

"Well, we're gonna head out, continue our chair search," Caroline says. "Nice to see you again, Nolan." She gives her friend a small smile. "See you tomorrow, Maya."

We wave goodbye, then fall back onto the couch, exhausted.

And worried.

And confused as fuck.

"So, what do we think?" The saleswoman reappears and beams down at us. "Is this one the winner?"

I glance over at Maya, and she nods almost imperceptibly.

"Load 'er up, Lauretta. We'll take it."

Chapter 15

MAYA

I steel myself as I pull open the door to Making Waves and step into the quiet boutique. We're scheduled to open in fifteen minutes, but I wanted to make sure I came in early so I could talk with River.

I've spent the last twenty-four hours worried about Caroline catching us at the furniture store. She promised me she wouldn't say anything to River before I could, and I promised I'd tell her today.

So, here I am, three coffees in hand, ready to tell my best friend I'm sleeping with her boyfriend's best friend after she warned me not to.

Caroline lifts her head from where she's standing at the register, likely going over the sketches in her notebook.

"Morning," she says as I set the coffees down in front of her. She reaches for the smallest cup, popping the lid off to help it cool down. I don't tell her it's probably fine since I spent the last ten minutes standing outside trying not to freak out over the email I woke up to.

The apartment I'm waiting on will be ready sooner than

expected. Sam and I can move in the weekend before his birthday if we're ready.

That's just two weeks away.

I'm ready to move into my own place. I want a space that's just for me and Sam.

But, if I'm being honest with myself, I'm going to miss Nolan.

And I'm not sure I'm ready to face that truth.

"How was your Saturday off?" Caroline asks.

I give her a look, and she smothers a laugh with her hand.

"Oh, good, you're here!" River claps her hands, skipping out of the back office like the psychotic morning person she is. "And you brought coffee."

I hold up a baggie. "And treats."

"You're the best." She smacks a kiss to my cheek and snatches the bag away, digging into the delicious baked goods. She takes a healthy bite of a blueberry muffin, then wipes her mouth on the back of her hand. "So, I heard you went furniture shopping with Nolan yesterday."

I snap my eyes to Caroline as my heart hammers in my chest.

Eyes wide, she shakes her head, telling me she didn't say a word.

"I thought you guys were doing that last Sunday and that's why you couldn't come hang with us."

Oh.

I exhale slowly. "We got busy doing other stuff last Sunday and then never got home early enough during the week to go before they closed."

She nods. "Makes sense. Did you find a couch you both love?"

"*Nolan* found a couch he loves. My opinion doesn't matter because I don't really live there. I was just there so he didn't buy something ugly."

She smacks her forehead "Right, duh. Sometimes I forget you're not staying in the building." She sticks her bottom lip out. "Which makes me super sad, by the way. I really love having you and my nephew so close."

"The new place isn't that far away."

"It's a lot farther than going up a few floors."

"True, but it's okay. Speaking of the new place…" I pull my phone from the purse, swiping past the lock screen, then navigating to my email. "I got an email this morning."

I hand it over to River, who sets her muffin on the counter.

She squeals with delight when she sees the good news. "You get to move in early!"

"What?" Caroline asks, snatching my phone from River's hands, scanning the email herself. "But what about Nolan?"

"What about him?" River asks. "He's not going with her."

"No, I mean what about—" She clamps her lips together, shaking her head, stopping herself from spilling the beans. "Never mind."

"Oooooh," River says, bobbing her head. "You mean are they still going to sleep together after Maya moves out?"

"Caroline!" I yell, glowering at her.

"It wasn't me!" she promises, holding her hands up in innocence.

River cackles loudly, clapping a few times. We stare at her as she slaps her thighs, still carrying on like a maniac.

When she finally calms down, she wipes at her eyes, brushing away the tears that have formed.

Then she pins me with a stare like she didn't just laugh

like a crazed person, her lips falling into a flat line.

"You're on my shitlist, Maya West."

I gulp because she means it. "H-How did you find out?"

"You're kidding, right?" She huffs, rolling her eyes. "You're my best friend. I've known you since we were eight —I know when you're getting dicked on the regular." She shrugs. "Plus, I went to knock on your door one day, wanting a girls' night, and heard you screaming Nolan's name in a way that told me he was anything but in trouble."

Heat fills my cheeks because I don't doubt it for a minute. I'm not exactly quiet in the bedroom when it comes to Nolan unless Sam is home.

"How long have you known?"

"Since…" She taps her chin. "Gosh, probably a couple of days after you guys came down for drinks. I'm assuming it started that night. You two wouldn't stop staring at each other the whole time."

"How would you know? You were shit-faced."

"I wasn't *that* drunk."

I lift my brow at her.

She waves her hand. "Fine, I was pretty drunk. But also, I spent a long time gazing at Dean like that before we finally got our shit together. I know what longing looks like when I see it."

"Why didn't you say anything?"

"Why didn't you?" She turns her glare on Caroline. "And why didn't *you*?"

"Hey, I just found out yesterday," she says. "We caught them practically dry-humping on one of the display couches."

"We were not dry-humping!"

"Uh-huh. Sure you weren't."

"We weren't," I mumble, then turn back to River. "I'm sorry I didn't tell you. I just didn't want you to be mad at me."

"Why would I be mad at you?"

"Because you told me not to get involved with him because he doesn't do relationships."

"I armed you with that knowledge, sure, but you're a grown-ass adult who can make her own decisions. Who you sleep with is none of my business. Besides, it would be hypocritical of me to judge you for acting on your urges with your hot-as-fuck roommate."

I chuckle. "True. So, you're not mad?"

She shakes her head. "Not at all. Do I worry about you? Yes, but that's my job as your best friend. It's also my job to support you no matter what dumb choice you make."

"You think what I'm doing is dumb?"

She twists her lips back and forth, then finally shakes her head. "No. But I think you think it's dumb."

I slam my brows together. "How?"

"Because you're hiding it. If you feel good about what you're doing, you don't hide it—especially not from the people who love you."

"I—"

Well, crap. She has me there.

It's not that I think what I'm doing with Nolan is wrong. It's not. Giving in to sexual urges is natural.

But do I think it's reckless? Yeah, a little.

Especially because I'm really starting to get used to him and because I'm more anxious about walking away from him than I am about moving into my new apartment.

I like what we have…and I don't want to let it go.

I want more.

I know that's not what we agreed to, and it's wrong of me to expect anything more.

If I were braver, I'd cut things off now before I get even more attached.

But I'm too selfish to do that.

"For what it's worth, I agree with River," Caroline says. "And I just want to say I know what it's like to fall for someone you're not supposed to fall for. It's scary and hard, and I'm here if you need to talk."

I want to correct her, tell her I'm not falling for Nolan.

But I'm not so sure that's accurate anymore.

Panic slams into my chest and I put my hand over my heart, trying to calm it.

Oh god. What the hell are we doing? Why did we think this was a good idea?

"Hey, I fell for someone I wasn't supposed to fall for either."

Caroline and I laugh.

"Please," Caroline says, "you and Dean never hated each other. You just couldn't get over yourselves long enough to see that."

River pulls a face. "Whatever." She reaches for my hand. "Listen, I'm not mad…but I do think you need to look deep in your heart and be honest with yourself. Then with Nolan. It'll make things easier when you show him the email."

She's right. Of course she's right.

I need to talk to Nolan about this.

How the hell am I going to tell him I'm falling in love with him?

191

"Hey." Nolan beams at me from his perch on his reading chair, long legs stretched out before him, his bare feet hanging off the edge because he's so tall. There's a book in his hands and he puts a finger between the pages to hold his spot. "How was your day?"

He looks so good sitting there in nothing but those black sweats that make me want to rub my thighs together. I can't help it when my feet carry me across the room and straight into his lap.

This isn't the first time I've found him reading in my room, and part of me likes to believe he spends his time in here because he misses me.

"Oh, so that's where we're going, huh? All right. I can get behind this. Thank god Sam's downstairs for a guitar lesson right now."

His fingers dig into my waist and he buries his face in my neck, kissing and sucking on all the spots he knows I like.

I rub against him like I'm sex-deprived, never mind the fact that he spent the morning between my legs before sending me off to work.

"You taste so good," he murmurs, licking at my skin. "I could get used to that."

I don't think he realizes he says it aloud.

If he does, it doesn't hit him the same way it hits me.

I don't know whether I'm thankful for that or upset by it.

I don't get the chance to dwell on it as his fingers find their way under my shirt. He pulls the material up my body, tossing it somewhere nearby. He unhooks my bra like he's an expert at it, and considering the number of times he's taken it off over the past few weeks, I guess he is.

He kisses my breasts until I'm writhing against him, then

he unbuttons my jeans, sliding his hand into my underwear. He presses a finger into me, then two, using his thumb to play with my clit.

When he adds a third one, I fall apart around him, collapsing into his arms as I come back down to earth.

I've died and gone straight to heaven with his arms wrapped tightly around me, his fingers ghosting up and down my bare back as he kisses me lazily, his lips coaxing me back to life.

"Need you," he mutters against me.

"Take me," I answer.

He lifts us off the chair long enough to lay me down on my back. He strips his sweats off, then pulls my jeans down and fits himself between my legs like he's always belonged there.

And really, he has.

He hooks my leg around his waist and slides into me with a grunt, his eyes never leaving mine as he makes lazy thrusts.

There's no rush, no hurried frenzy like the one that's been between us.

We take our time.

We don't speak.

Don't make a sound.

Not when another orgasm races through me and not when he empties himself inside of me.

Something passes between us.

Something that scares me.

That scares him.

And I know in that moment we are completely screwed.

Chapter 16

NOLAN

Maya told me yesterday River knows about us, so I wasn't surprised when my phone started blowing up on the jobsite today.

Dean: I FUCKING KNEW IT!

Dean: "Nothing," he said.

Dean: Nothing my ass!

Dean: Fucker.

Me: Are you done having a hissy fit?

Dean: No.

Dean: Yes.

Dean: Beers tonight?

Me: Hole in One? 7?

Dean: Sounds good.

Dean: You owe me several drinks.

Dean: GIF of someone shaking head

"That your girlfriend again?" Jake asks, legs swinging back and forth as we take a break on the bed of my truck.

"No, Dean—though sometimes he feels like my girlfriend."

Jake laughs. "Best friends can be pains in the dick...much like girlfriends."

"You ain't lying there." I lift my hard hat and run my hand through my hair before putting it back in place. "He found out about my...roommate."

The word feels like acid in my mouth.

Wrong and painful.

Jake whistles. "He pissed?"

"I think he's more upset his girlfriend found out before he did."

He laughs. "Men can say they hate drama and gossip all they want, but they don't like being left out of it either."

"That sounds exactly like Dean. He's almost as bad about gossip as some of the old ladies in our apartment building." I shake my head. "I still love the asshole though."

"We all have that one friend we love just as much as we want to smack them upside the head."

He's not wrong there.

The boss signals break is over, and we get back to the grind. I do everything in my power to put my thoughts solely on my job and not think about Maya, but of course she slips through the cracks.

She's *been* slipping through them for weeks.

When we're not together, all I can do is think of her. When we are together, all I want to do is touch her.

It's becoming a problem that's getting too big to ignore.

Before I know it, Jake's tapping my shoulder, telling me we're done for the day. I load up my equipment and check my phone. It's already six thirty, so I'll have to skip heading home to wash up before meeting with Dean.

Sitting in my truck, I swap my work shirt for a flannel and pull my phone out to shoot off a text to Maya.

Only my fingers hover over the keyboard.

Why the hell am I telling her where I'm at and when I'll be home? She's not my girlfriend. I don't need to do that. She doesn't need to know everything going on with me.

It's just fucking sex.

Annoyed by myself, I toss my phone into the passenger seat before setting off for the bar. Twenty minutes later, I'm parking and talking myself into walking in and getting the inquisition over with.

I finally convince myself to get out of the truck and walk inside, immediately signaling to Donny for a drink.

He sets a tumbler of scotch in front of me along with a beer.

"Looks like you could use it," he says, then he lifts his chin. "'Sup, Dean?"

"Hey, Donny." Dean slides onto the stool next to me. "I'll take the same thing he has. This son of a bitch is paying tonight."

"Coming right up."

We don't talk until Donny delivers Dean's drinks before moving down to the other end of the bar where his boyfriend is.

It's a Monday, so the place is more quiet than usual.

I'm relieved. I don't think I could have dealt with any sort of crowd tonight.

"So," Dean says, lifting his scotch glass, "to making dumb decisions like banging our temporary roommates."

We're both aware Maya isn't just my roommate.

The more painful realization? She hasn't been in a long

time. I don't know exactly when it happened, but she's wormed her way inside a part of me I keep locked up tight.

And so has her kid.

I lift my glass anyway, clinking it against his. We toss our drinks back.

Dean grimaces, wiping his mouth with the back of his hand, shaking his head. "Fuck, I hate that shit. I don't know how you drink it."

"I figured you'd like it. It's an acquired taste…like you."

He shoves my shoulder. "Fuck you very much. And fuck you for not being honest about Maya."

I sigh. "In all fairness, the night we met, it was nothing then."

I tell him what happened while he and River were running late. How I had no idea who she was. How offering her a place to live was based on pure, innocent intentions.

How I never meant to fall into bed with her, and it's the truth.

Maya was firmly put into the *off limits* category in my mind.

But…then she wasn't. And I was fucked from that moment on…and not just literally.

Dean blows out a breath, running his hands through his hair.

"Wow." He laughs. "We're going to need another shot to celebrate this shit."

"What? Why? Celebrate what?"

He claps me on the back. "This monumental moment."

I shrug his touch off, scowling at him. "Just fucking out with it already."

"You're in love with her."

197

"The fuck I am," I say at once.

And the asshole's grin grows.

"What?" I bark, and he laughs.

He fucking *laughs*.

"Swear to god...I'm leaving."

I push myself up off the stool, reaching into my back pocket, ready to throw some cash down and bail.

"Oh, shut up, you big baby." Dean shoves me back down. "Quit being so dramatic."

"I'm not being dramatic."

"I say the word love and you're ready to literally run away? That's not dramatic?" He raises a sharp brow. "That's what I thought," he says when I don't respond. "Now, how about we react to this like rational adults, huh?"

I scrub a hand over my face, sighing loudly as I drop my head to the counter, banging it a few times, not giving a shit how sticky it is. "There's nothing to fucking talk about. I'm not in love with her."

I'm not.

I can't be.

If I'm in love with her, that gives her power over me—power like my mom had over my dad. And I don't want anyone to have that sort of hold on me.

"You poor, poor delusional man." He pats my back. "It's okay, you know. You can love her. It's not the end of the world. In fact, I knew this day would come eventually."

"You didn't know shit."

He shakes with laughter. "Cheer up. At least you didn't fall for a girl who sometimes makes you question if she could murder you and not lose an ounce of sleep over it."

That elicits a small chuckle from me.

"Dumbass," I mutter, lifting my head. "River's fucking scary as hell sometimes."

"Oh, you don't even know." He takes a pull off his beer. "But it's kind of exhilarating never knowing how she's going to react to something. Keeps shit fun, you know?"

"You talk like you've been dating for years, not half a year."

"Sometimes it feels like it's been decades." He says it like he's exasperated by her, but he's not. He loves her wholly, always willing to put everything on the line for her.

We don't say anything for a long time, sipping our beers while I try not to panic.

"How do you do it?"

"Do what?" he says. "That thing with my tongue she loves? Let me grab a lemon from Donny. It's best if I demonstrate it."

He lifts his hand and I smack it out of the air, waving Donny off.

"No. I mean, how do you...you know..." I run my tongue over my dry lips. "Love her? Aren't you scared she's going to break you?"

"Oh." His eyes grow serious and he sighs, dropping his shoulders. "Honestly? I don't know she's not going to break me, and sometimes that fucks me up. But the moments where it doesn't...they're my favorite moments of all time." A lazy grin forms. "It's worth it for all those moments."

"What if..." Emotion clogs my throat, hitting me out of nowhere. I sling back the rest of my beer, shaking it off.

"She leaves?" Dean asks, understanding the question. "Then she leaves. Don't get me wrong, it's going to fucking wreck me and I'll wish I were dead, but it's not going to make me want to take back any of the in-between, you know? If I have those memories to fade away into, I'll survive it."

I wonder if that's how my dad felt.

We didn't talk about my mom leaving much. We didn't need to. I saw the emptiness in his eyes every day.

But now I wish I would have asked him how he kept going on…if he had those moments too.

"Listen, I've known you a long time—perhaps too fucking long if you ask me." Bold of him to make that statement. "I was there when your mom left. I saw what it did to your pops. I saw what it did to you. But, man, there was nothing that could have been done differently. You didn't make her leave—she did it on her own. Your father didn't make her leave either. It was her decision. You can't hold that against anyone but your mother. You can't keep pushing love away just because you're afraid it's going to hurt, because trust me, it'll hurt even when it's good."

He finishes off the last swig of his beer.

"But it's worth it, Nolan," he adds quietly. "It's all worth it."

I switched to water shortly after Dean dropped his words of wisdom and drove the long way home.

I've been sitting in my truck in the parking garage for thirty minutes now.

Thirty-one.

Thirty-two.

Thirty-three.

I can't seem to make myself get out.

Not even when my phone buzzes.

Maya: Just making sure you're okay?

I don't answer her.

Thirty-four.

Thirty-five.

I'm stuck, Dean's words filtering through my head.

I understood what he was saying about the in-between moments.

But are they worth the inevitable heartache? Is it worth it to put yourself on the line? If it is, how am I supposed to know if she's the person I should do it for? Is there a sign I should be looking for? A clue? A moment where it's all supposed to click into place?

I'm pissed at myself for even thinking about this at all.

We weren't supposed to get involved, and I definitely wasn't supposed to get attached to her. But every time I look at the date, a little more panic sets in. She's leaving soon, and I don't fucking want her to.

I hate that I don't want her to.

When forty-five minutes pass by, I figure it's time to go in. I can't hide out here forever.

The elevator is slow, but the stairs are even slower, so I take those. By the time I finally hit my floor, it's almost ten, and I'm sure Maya is likely already in bed.

It'll be the first night we haven't spent together since we started this thing.

Maybe that's for the best though.

Maybe we need the space. The perspective.

Maybe a pause is what we need to ensure we're not getting too caught up in each other.

Dean is wrong. I'm not in love with her. I'm infatuated, addicted to the sex.

That's all it is.

I push open the door, making sure I'm as quiet as possible. Sam's already in bed for the night, and I don't want to wake him.

I don't want to wake Maya either.

The apartment is noiseless as I toe off my boots, then stop in the kitchen for a glass of water.

I guzzle it down, refilling it once more before padding down the hall to my bedroom.

Maya's door is open, and I can't seem to stop myself from peeking inside.

She's on her side, facing the door.

And she's staring right at me.

She doesn't move, and I'm pretty sure she stops breathing altogether as her eyes find mine.

I itch to go to her. To bury my face in her neck and roll her on her back, finding my place between her legs that feels like heaven and a sin all at once.

But I don't.

Instead, I roll my shoulders back and turn for my bedroom.

I don't know what's louder—the click of my door or her gasp.

Chapter 17

MAYA

I don't know what happened the night Nolan came home late, but whatever it was, something changed.

One day everything was fine, and I even thought we had shared something special. Then nothing was good again.

Nothing has been the same for days. He barely looks at me and hardly says a word. I still haven't even had the chance to tell him about the apartment being available earlier than expected. He's been avoiding me, and it's exhausting. I am more than over it.

This morning when I got up to make breakfast, his bedsheets were cold, which meant he was long gone.

I tried to push the haunted gaze I saw on his face out of my head and focus on taking care of Sam, but it's been hard. He was late for school again today—the third time in as many days—and as I pulled away from the school, I promptly received an angry call from his principal about his repeated tardiness.

I didn't even have it in me to argue with him about it. He was right anyway.

When I show up at the boutique every day, I paste on a smile Caroline and River seem to buy and lock myself in the storeroom for the rest of my shift until I have to pick up Sam.

I've declined a coffee date and invitation to dinner from them, always rushing home to see if Nolan's there waiting, that lazy grin back on his face.

It's not, and at this point, I'm just going through the motions.

When Sam asked for help on his homework tonight, I jumped at the request, a reprieve from thinking about where things went so wrong.

We have our heads bent together when Nolan comes through the door later than he normally does.

"Dude, Nolan, you missed breakfast this morning. Mom made pancakes," Sam declares before he even has the door closed.

Nolan gives him a tight-lipped smile, not bothering to glance in my direction. "That's nice, bud."

He slips his boots off, then rises to his full height, heading right for the fridge.

"I made pork chops tonight. There's a plate in the microwave for you."

He nods but doesn't say anything as he dips his head, shuffling things around, sighing.

"Something wrong?" I ask.

"Where's my cherry PowerUp?"

"It should be behind the milk." I push off the stool, going to help him look.

"Perfectly capable of pushing a gallon of milk out of the way," he snaps, causing me to shrink back. "It's not there."

"Um..." Sam says, pulling our attention his way. He

scrunches his face up, and I already know what's coming next before he says it. "I took it to school with me this morning and drank it."

"It's okay, kiddo," I tell him.

"No, it's not okay." He slams the fridge closed, gaze angry and sharp. "That was mine."

I snap my head to Nolan, narrowing my eyes at him. "It's just a drink, Nolan. He didn't know better."

"I'm sorry," Sam says quietly.

"It's okay," I tell him again. "Just make sure you ask next time. Why don't you go put your homework in your backpack before you forget?"

His eyes bounce back and forth between me and Nolan, the worry clear in his stare.

Patrick and I had our fair share of problems, but we never fought in front of Sam, and I don't have any intentions of fighting with Nolan in front of him either.

With his shoulders sagging, Sam gathers his things and trudges down the hall.

As soon as he's around the corner, I whirl on Nolan.

"What the hell is your problem?" I seethe, poking a finger into his chest. "Don't you ever talk to my kid like that again. You need to apologize to him."

He mutters something I don't quite catch, but I know it's not good.

"What did you just say?"

He gnashes his teeth together. "I said, maybe your kid should be a little more respectful of shit that isn't his. I found one of my books under the couch this morning too, and there were Cheeto fingerprints on the pages I *know* didn't come from me."

I see the regret in his eyes with every word he speaks. He's not lashing out at Sam. Not really. He's lashing out at me. I just don't know why.

Nevertheless, the things he's saying about my child are pissing me off.

Sam doesn't deserve his ire.

I step into him. "I don't know what your problem is, but you need to get a grip and stop blaming a twelve-year-old for whatever is going on in that thick head of yours."

"Nothing is going on other than I'm tired of not having my space to myself."

I lift a brow. "Really?"

"Really." He doesn't back down. If anything, he doubles down on his convictions…whatever the fuck they are.

"Well, lucky for you, you don't have to worry about that any longer. We're moving out—next weekend."

He swallows once. Twice.

And then, he nods, casting his eyes away from me.

"Good."

The word is final and sounds eerily like a goodbye.

"Good," I echo.

"I think that's for the best."

"I do too."

He steps back, then around me, making sure not to brush against me as he passes by. "Let me know if you need help moving."

I don't move a muscle.

If I move, this is real.

We're done.

It's over.

If I move, I'm going to break.

"Well, that should be the last of it."

Cooper sets the heavy box down with a grunt, then wipes the sweat off his forehead.

"Thank you, Coop. I know I took you away from a day of gaming, but I appreciate it so much more than you know."

"It's not a problem at all. Besides, if I said no, I'm pretty sure Caroline would withhold sex from me for at least a week."

"Two!" she calls from my bedroom, where she's hanging clothes up in my closet with River.

For the second move in as many months, Sam's at his dad's. Though it would be nice to have him here for the help, it'll be good to have one more night to myself before I have to go pick him up tomorrow.

This past week has been one of the most tiring of my life. Who knew avoiding someone requires so much energy?

I boxed all of my and Sam's things back up throughout the week and asked Cooper and Dean to help me move.

This morning when I walked out of the apartment with my last box in hand, Nolan was nowhere to be found.

We haven't said a word to each other since I told him I was moving out, and I still don't know what went wrong.

One day he was fine; the next he wasn't.

It was like a switch flipped.

"Hey," Cooper says in a low voice. "You okay?"

"Huh?"

He rubs his hand over the back of his neck. "You sort of drifted away for a minute…"

His pale green eyes are full of worry, and I love the guy for being so concerned.

I clear my throat. "I'm good."

But even I know my smile wobbles.

He flicks his gaze toward Dean, who is in the kitchen unpacking the essentials, then steps toward me, keeping his voice down. "Caroline mentioned you still haven't talked to Nolan, and he's not here today…"

I finally broke down and told River and Caroline about what happened. I had to physically restrain River so she didn't run out of the boutique to go beat Nolan up for breaking my heart the way he did.

It's my fault though. I should have never let my feelings get involved.

It was supposed to be just sex, and I'm the one who broke that promise.

"He's busy with work is all. They're starting a new project, so he has a lot to do."

Cooper doesn't look convinced, but he lets it go.

He nods, stepping back. "Okay. Just…I know I'm not Caroline or whatever, but I've spent the past ten years being best friends with a chick, and I'm a good listener. So, if you need anything…"

I wrap my arms around him, surprising us both.

"Thank you, Cooper," I whisper, choking back my emotions the best I can.

I haven't cried over Nolan yet, and I'm not about to start now—not with an apartment full of all our mutual friends.

He squeezes me back. "Always."

I push away, squaring my shoulders. "All right. Let's get this couch moved, huh?"

We order a pizza for lunch and work four more hours getting everything set up how I want it, Dean and Cooper moving my couch and TV around no less than three times each.

It's dusk when they all pile out, and I'm more than ready for them to go. I have a brand-new garden tub and a fresh bottle of wine calling my name.

A few minutes after I close my door on River and Dean, there's a knock.

I pull it open, surprised to see Dean standing on the other side.

"Forget something?"

"No." He shoves his hands into his pockets, shuffling his feet, kicking at the dirt that isn't there. "Well, yeah. Maybe. I..." He blows out a breath. "I, uh... This might be my fault, Maya."

My lips pull into a frown. "What do you mean?"

"I think I might have freaked Nolan out."

I tip my head to the side, waiting for him to continue.

"I didn't mean to. It's just..." He shrugs. "He's so in his head, you know? So worried he's going to become his father and die with a broken heart. Still so angry at his mom. But I thought maybe hearing it would help him pull his head out of his ass."

His words are coming out so fast I'm having a hard time keeping up.

"What'd you tell him, Dean?"

"I told him he's in love with you."

"You...what?" My head is spinning. Or is that the world? Either way, I grip the doorframe to keep steady. "Why?"

Another shrug. "Because it's true."

"Dean, I—"

He shakes his head, halting my words. "Don't. Don't try to pull that same shit and deny it. He's in love with you, and if the way you've been moping around for the past week is any sign, you're in love with him too."

My mouth opens, ready to argue with him.

But…he's right.

I'm in love with Nolan.

I have no idea when it happened, but it snuck right up on me, and as much as I've been trying, I don't know how to make it stop. It hurts to love him, but I think it'll hurt to not love him even more.

"Anyway," Dean continues, "he kind of freaked a bit at first. Then he seemed to accept it, maybe even embrace it. I have no fucking idea what happened between then and now, but I can't help thinking it was something I said to make him push you away."

His shoulders are hunched and his eyes are full of so many apologies that don't need to be said.

No matter what Dean said to Nolan, none of this is his fault. Nolan is an adult, and how he chose to react is solely on his shoulders. If running is the way he decides to take care of things, that's on him.

"You're a good friend, Dean, and Nolan is lucky to have you."

He puffs his chest out. "Pfft. I know."

"None of this is on you, though, and I think I'm starting to realize it's not on me either. It's on Nolan. If you were right about him…"

I trail off, the words caught in my throat.

"About him being…" I try again, but they won't come out.

210

I shake my head. "If you were right, then it's up to Nolan what he's going to do about it. If this is how he deals, this is it, and I'll accept that."

Dean's face falls, not liking that answer. "But what about" —he points between us—"this? River? Us?"

"If I can co-parent with my ex-husband, I think I'll be just fine co-friending with Nolan."

His eyes search mine, and I try to convey as much reassurance as I can.

He accepts what he sees with a dip of his chin. "Okay. But if I need to go kick his ass, just say the word. He certainly has it coming."

I laugh, imagining the kids' reaction to Dean showing up at school with a black eye. "Have I mentioned lately how glad I am that you and River finally got over your shit? She's lucky you put up with her."

"Thank you! That's what I've been trying to tell her. I'm practically Prince Fucking Charming."

"I don't think Prince Charming's middle name is fucking."

He gives me a mischievous grin. "It is in my version." He winks. "Night, Maya."

"Good night, Dean."

I close the door behind him, sinking against it, the weight of the last week taking its toll.

I'm worn out.

From moving.

From pretending I'm okay.

From acting like my heart isn't on fire.

I skip my bath, but not the bottle of wine.

When my head hits the pillow and I reach across the empty bed, the tears finally come.

Chapter 18

NOLAN

It's ironic, really, me sitting at Hole in One slinging back shots.

The night I met Maya, I tried to convince her I wasn't there to nurse a broken heart.

Tonight, that's exactly what I'm doing.

I couldn't bear the thought of going home to an empty apartment again, so I'm sitting on a barstool trying to drown my sorrows. This is the third night this week Donny has fed me drinks.

I'm starting to feel a buzz, but it's nowhere near the one I felt whenever Maya was there.

It never is.

If this is even a fraction of what my father felt when my mother left, I have no idea how the old man held out as long as he did.

I'm tired because I'm not sleeping. Being in my bed without her doesn't feel right. I'm hungry because I'm not eating because I can't, and my head is throbbing because it's waging a constant battle with my heart.

If this is being in love, no thanks.

It's fucking exhausting.

The worst part of it all? This is my own damn fault.

I knew the moment I let my frustration out and directed it at Sam I'd fucked up. Deep down I didn't mean to yell at the kid, but I couldn't stop the words coming out of my mouth. I wanted to hurt her before she could hurt me.

It's what I do. What I've always done.

And I'm a fucking moron for doing so.

Being without her these last few weeks...I know that now.

Dean was right about the moments. They're all I have to cling to, and I find myself escaping into them more than I probably should since I'm the one who did the leaving like a coward.

Someone bumps into me, jostling the fresh shot of whiskey in my hand.

It's rare I ever do shots, but I needed them today.

"What the..."

The words die on my lips when Dean comes into view and a shadow falls over me as Cooper slips onto the stool on my other side.

I tighten my hand around the shot glass and toss the liquid back, then I run the back of my hand across my lips.

"What."

It's not a question. Not really.

It's more of a *Fuck off*, and they both know it. They just don't give a shit.

Dean chuckles. "Good to see you too, buddy."

I've been avoiding him. Hell, I've been avoiding everyone. I'm grumpy and agitated. No sense in making everyone else suffer too.

"What are you doing here?"

"Donny called me," Dean answers, nodding toward the bartender, who sets two drinks in front of the guys.

I glare at him. "The fuck, Donny?"

He holds his hands up. "Just doing my job."

"Sticking your nose where it doesn't belong?"

"Caring about my customers, especially the ones I like the most." He pours me another shot. "That one is on the house. You're welcome."

I tip it back, grimacing as my stomach turns.

I need to slow down. I haven't eaten today, and I'm not used to drinking like this.

Like he can read my mind, Donny sets a glass of water in front of me.

"You're officially cut off," he says, then he stalks away.

I don't argue. I don't have the energy.

It's probably for the best though. The last thing I need is to get wasted and do something stupid like call Maya and tell her I'm in love with her.

"Hey, Dean?" Cooper says over me. "How you been lately?"

"Oh, you know, not too bad. Busy with work, but not too busy to help a friend move or go to a birthday party for the coolest kid ever."

I grind my teeth together until it hurts.

Then I do it some more.

They think they're so fucking clever.

"Moving? A birthday party? Wow, those both sound like pretty big deals."

"They are. It's important to be there for people you care about, though, so I made sure I didn't bail. Especially since my friend...I don't know, man. She's so sad. She tried to put on a brave face, tried to pretend she wasn't crying on the inside. But I could see it still."

"Why's she sad?"

"Because some asshole wouldn't pull his head out of his ass and tell her he's in love with her."

I suck down half my water before slamming the glass back down on the counter.

"Hardy har-har. You guys are a real riot. You should start your own comedy troupe."

"Why? You're the one who's a joke."

I'm so fucking pathetic I can't even summon my anger.

He's right.

I am a joke.

Why can't I just tell Maya I love her? Why can't I let go of all my reservations and be happy? Because I'm scared to end up like my father? Rotting away with a chip on my shoulder?

But isn't that what I'm doing anyway by not ever letting myself be truly happy?

Dean takes a swig of his beer, then sighs, setting it back down on the counter with force. "You know, you've done some dumb shit over the years. Like the time you thought it would be funny to try to light a fart on fire and ended up setting your curtains on fire instead. Or the time we went on a double date at the carnival and you ate six hot dogs before getting on the Twister. You puked on yourself and on me, leading to us both getting dumped."

"And I haven't known you that long," Cooper says, "but remember our Christmas dinner when you had a little too much to drink and decided to go swimming out in Lake Swanson and almost got hypothermia?"

"See? Some real stupid shit." Dean shakes his head. "But you have never, ever done anything as dumb as letting Maya go."

"You think I don't fucking know that?" I growl. "You think I'm not aware of that?"

"Honestly, since you didn't bother to show up to Sam's birthday party, yeah, I was worried you didn't realize just how big of a dick you are."

The disgust and bile rise in my throat.

Dean sent me no less than ten texts when I didn't show this past weekend.

But I couldn't do it. Couldn't face them.

"You being there meant a lot to him, and you couldn't even be bothered to put your shit with Maya aside and show up for him." He laughs sardonically. "You've spent a lot of time pushing away everyone who could ever hurt you so you don't become your father, but did you ever consider that's moot since you're more like your mother than you realize?"

His words slam into my gut like a fist.

I abandoned Maya. I abandoned Sam.

I've abandoned everyone in my life when they got too close.

I was never in danger of becoming my father because I've always been my mother.

"Fuck!"

The scream hurls through my chest, echoing around the near-empty bar.

Donny's wide eyes find us and a few heads turn our way, but nobody makes a move to see what's the matter.

Cooper pats me on the back. "Let it out, man. Just let it all out. We all make mistakes. We all screw up at this love thing now and again."

I hang my head between my shoulders, ready to puke for the second time tonight.

I don't want to be my mother *or* my father.

All I want to be is Maya's.

I just have to figure out how to make her see that too.

Every morning my alarm goes off, I lie there as long as I possibly can. Opening my eyes means facing the reality of an empty bed.

Maya has been gone for two weeks now, and I've been clutching the edge of survival for just as long.

My sleep is getting worse, but at least I've progressed to eating one meal a day. It's all I can muster, but I'll take the small victory.

I'm miserable as fuck, and I still don't know how to fix it.

I'm not sure how I'm supposed to go about professing my love for someone when I've never been in love before. I've never even come close to it.

Can't someone just write a book on this? That'd be so much easier. A nice how-to guide on groveling. I'd buy the shit out of that book.

"Yo, Brooks," I hear over the noise of my welder as Jake taps me on the shoulder.

I push my helmet off. "What's up?"

"Lunch, man. We're going to the diner again and you're coming with."

"No, thanks." I shove my helmet back down, turning back to my work.

He yanks on me again. "Sorry, man. You're going."

"I'm not."

Another pull, and I finally wrench my helmet off again.

"I said I wasn't going."

He steps back, holding his hands up. "Dude, it's not my decision. I'd love to leave your crabby ass here, but the boss called and said we need to clear out. He has someone coming in to look at the place and doesn't want us riffraff bothering them."

Fuck.

I don't want to go out with the crew. I'm more than happy to sit in my truck and stew, the same thing I've been doing for two weeks now.

We started on the project replacing Maya's old building on the day she moved out. One last *Fuck you* from the universe.

I sigh. "Fine. But I'm not driving your ass. Get your own ride." I shoulder past him, sending him stumbling.

"Love you too, buddy," he calls to my back, laughing.

I toss my tools into my truck, then yank off my welding jacket. It's freezing outside and I'm wearing nothing but a white short-sleeved tee, but I don't bother putting on anything else.

I welcome the cold.

It's how my world feels anyway.

The drive to The Gravy Train isn't long, and I'm pulling into the parking lot long before I want to. I could go home and avoid facing the crew, but home reminds me of Maya and everything I pushed away.

At least the diner doesn't…too much.

I swing the door open, and the moment I do, I hear it.

Her laugh.

My eyes find the source of the sound, and all the air is stolen from my lungs. Her head is tossed back, shoulders shaking as she laughs at something Sam said.

She's gorgeous. Stunning.

And for the briefest moment in time, she was all mine.

I want to charge over there, tell her I'm an idiot and I screwed up and I want her back in my bed...my home...my life...more than anything else I've ever wanted, but I can't seem to make myself move.

I'm too fucking scared.

The urge to run away hits me again. I find my feet, spinning on my heel to bolt, but I'm stopped.

"No way." Jake shoves me back inside. "We're having lunch and you will enjoy every damn minute of it."

I could fight him off, shove back, but all it would do is draw attention to us, and that's the last thing I want. With reluctance, I shuffle into the restaurant and get in line behind the other guys.

I can feel her eyes on me and I revel in it, having missed it way too much the past few weeks.

"Nolan!"

I slam my eyes closed, taking a steadying breath, then paste on a beaming smile.

I turn to Sam. "Hey, shithead. What's up?"

"Not much. I finally beat that big boss we couldn't get past."

"Nice. Sad I couldn't be there to help."

I apologized to him the night I yelled, and luckily he forgave me. I've grown fond of him over the last few months, and Maya leaving would have hurt even more if I'd known Sam left mad at me too.

"Yeah. Me too. You missed my birthday party this weekend." He shrugs, then slides his hands into his pockets, hanging his head. "But it's cool. Mom said you had to work, so I get it. Just wish you could have come."

Regret twists in my gut.

Fuck, I'm an asshole.

Seeing now how much I hurt him fucks me up in a way I wasn't expecting, and my chest tightens with emotion.

I swallow it down, clearing my throat. "I'm sorry."

Another shrug. "It's okay."

"Why, uh, why aren't you in school?"

"Skip day." He points to his mom, who is watching us with a sharp gaze. Our eyes collide, and I can't breathe all over again. "Mom's over there. I have to go to the bathroom."

He squeezes past me, leaving me standing there like a fool while everyone stares at me.

"Go talk to her, man." Jake gives me a gentle shove. "Apologize to her for whatever you did."

I glare at him. "How do you know I did anything?"

"Man, I've been married for five years now. You think that relationship didn't come with its struggles before we finally fixed our shit for good? I've been you. I know what you're going through." He juts out his chin toward Maya. "Just like I know you had better fix it soon because women like her don't come around often."

He doesn't know how right he is.

I knew she was special the first moment I saw her. I didn't get how much until later.

Now I fear I might be too late.

He gives me another prod, jostling me forward.

I straighten my shoulders, deciding to get it over with because at this point it would be more awkward if I didn't.

I take slow, intentional steps toward her.

Her eyes track my every move, her throat working as I get closer.

I stop at the end of her table, and I swear for a moment I can hear how hard her heart is beating.

Or maybe that's mine.

"Hey."

Hey? HEY? God, could I be lamer?

She lifts one of her sculpted brows. "Hey."

Her voice is icy, dripping with sarcasm.

She thinks I sound like an idiot too.

"Do you mind?" I point to the booth.

She waves her hand. "Go right ahead."

I slip into the spot across from her, noticing the way she backs up to avoid our knees brushing together. It reminds me of all the time we've spent sitting like this, finding any excuse to touch each other under the table where nobody could see us.

"I'm sorry I missed the party."

She chokes out a laugh, though there's not even a hint of humor in it. "Tell that to my son who was excited to show you the progress he made on his video game."

"I did."

She crosses her arms over her chest. "You know, Nolan, I can live with you ignoring me, but I can't deal with you hurting my kid. Sam loves you. He doesn't deserve that."

"You're right. He doesn't. I'm an asshole."

"A giant asshole."

221

"I'm a giant asshole."

The corners of her lips twitch, but she puts a stop to it fast, turning her gaze out the window.

We sit in silence, me tapping my fingers against the table in a nervous manner, her staring outside, pretending I'm not sitting across from her.

"So, uh," I start when I can't take it any longer, "how'd the move go?"

Like an ass, I volunteered to work the weekend she moved into her new place. I couldn't be there when she left. Couldn't watch her walk away.

"Fine."

"Do you like your new place?"

"It's fine."

"How are you?"

She drags her gray eyes back to me, and there's no mistaking the pain rippling in them, or the tiredness. Her eyes are puffy and dark, like she's not been sleeping well. I wonder if it's because of me.

"Fine, Nolan. I'm fine."

She's anything but fine, and we both know it.

She's hurting like I'm hurting.

I lean across the table and she matches my movement, though I'm not sure she even notices she does it.

I run my tongue over my lips, trying to find the words to say to her as she stares at me with a mix of curiosity and trepidation.

"Maya, I—"

"Hey, Mom," Sam says, interrupting us. Maya sits back, putting distance between us once again. "Can we get ice cream next?"

"Sure can, kiddo. Whatever you want."

I tilt my head, surprised.

She shrugs. "We do it every year around his birthday. I pull him out of school for a day and we have fun."

She tosses her hair over her shoulder and scoots out of the booth, ending our conversation.

I stand too, and a wave of awkwardness washes over us.

We don't know what to say, what to do. We stand there staring at one another like we've never met before. Like I don't know what she feels like...tastes like.

It's painful.

"Hey, Brooks! Food's here," Jake calls out, saving me.

I give him a nod, then turn back to Maya, who looks like she wants to stay and run all at the same time.

"Well, uh, it was good to see you," I say, like she's an old friend and not the girl who holds my heart in the palm of her hand.

She sighs, disappointed. "Yeah. You too."

"Later, shithead."

Sam rolls his eyes at me. "Are you coming to my talent show still? It's Friday night and I won't be playing a Bob Seger song."

I smirk. Dean was *not* happy with me for that one. "Yep. Wouldn't miss it."

Maya sends me a look saying *Don't you dare bail on him again.*

"I promise," I tell him, reassuring them both.

I hate the relief that floods his eyes.

I put that there, that doubt. I never wanted to get attached to the kid in the first place, and here I am feeling like absolute dog shit because I hurt him.

I'm sick to my stomach over it.

Jake whistles, signaling to me again.

"I better go before he comes over here and tries to spoon-feed me or something."

Before I can think about it too much, I lean into Maya and press a kiss to her cheek, inhaling her scent, which is slowly disappearing from my sheets. I linger longer than I should, but I can't seem to talk myself into walking away.

"I still need you," I whisper.

There's a hitch in her breath, and I pull back before I haul her into my arms and kiss her until we're both dizzy.

She gives me a small smile and rushes Sam from the restaurant.

She looks back at me twice, and I cling to the hope that gives me.

Chapter 19

MAYA

When Friday night rolls around, I can still feel Nolan's lips against my cheek.

I still need you.

It's been on repeat in my head for days now in that gravelly voice of his. I hear it everywhere. In the shower. In the car.

Amidst the cold loneliness of the night.

It's amazing how you can know someone for such a short amount of time and get so used to them that when they leave, your entire world is flipped around.

That's how I feel without Nolan.

I've been having trouble sleeping since I moved into my new place. Well, if I'm honest, the trouble started before that. But since we moved, it's gotten worse.

It's not the apartment, which is nice.

It's *him*.

It's what we had.

What I miss more than I thought was possible.

When we agreed to just sex, I meant it then. It was a means to a release. That was it.

He warned me too, said he didn't do attachments. I should have stopped things when I started falling, but I couldn't.

I didn't want to stop.

I just wanted him.

And despite everything, I *still* want him, even though I shouldn't.

I still need you.

If he still needs me, why isn't he here? Why isn't he busting down my door and proclaiming his love for me? Why isn't he showing up and being there?

If he's waiting on me to go running to him, he'll keep waiting. I had a one-sided relationship before, and I refuse to go down that path again no matter how much my heart is hurting.

"Mom! Have you seen my lucky pick?"

He has a lucky pick? "No. Is it not with your guitar?"

He and Dean have been practicing the guitar a few nights a week for almost two months now. He can successfully play four entire songs. I know this because he keeps playing *just* those four songs.

I love my son and I'm thankful Dean bought him a guitar for his birthday, but if I have to hear "Brown Eyed Girl" one more time, his guitar is going to find a new home in the Dumpster.

"No!" he calls back.

I slip my mascara wand back into the tube and give my hair one last fluff. I made sure to pick an outfit that makes me appear older. I always hate school functions because of the judgmental looks I get from the parents for being so young.

But honestly, I don't need the outfit tonight. The lack of sleep and bags under my eyes age me at least five years.

Who knew heartache had such an effect?

I switch off the bathroom light and make my way to Sam's bedroom. He's digging around in his dresser frantically, dropping to his hands and knees to check under it.

I cross my arms, leaning against the door. "Wild guess, but did you check your pocket?"

He groans, rolling his eyes at me. "Come on, Mom." He jams his hand into his pocket. "I'm not that du—" Pink flushes across his cheeks. "Oh."

I laugh. "Are you about ready then?"

"Yep."

But I hear the quiver in his voice.

He's nervous to play in front of a crowd, and I don't blame him. He's braver than me, that's for damn sure. I can't even say *I love you* to someone, and I'm a grown-ass adult.

"All right. Let's hit the road so we can get some decent parking. Your Aunt River and Dean are meeting us there."

"And Nolan, right?"

My heart squeezes at the mention of the man who holds it in the palm of his hand. "Yep."

I hope he doesn't hear the quiver in my voice too. "Come on."

He grabs his guitar and I grab my purse, then we head out to my car.

He's quiet on the drive, and I keep the radio low in case he wants to talk.

"Can I ask you something?"

"You ask me anything you want, except for a million

dollars. Not because I wouldn't give it to you, but because I don't have it."

He smiles. "It's not money."

"Oh, thank god." I wink. "What's up, kiddo?"

"Did you and Nolan break up because of me?"

If I weren't driving a car with my kid in it, I'd stop breathing right on the spot. But since I can't, I push through, exhaling slowly.

"Why…" The words are lodged in my throat, so I lick my lips to try again. "Why do you think Nolan and I were dating?"

He scoffs. "I have eyes."

"Really? Then why do you have such a hard time picking your socks up off the floor if you can see them lying there?"

"I said I have eyes, not gumption."

I smash my lips together, trying not to laugh. I didn't even realize he knew the word gumption. He should really stop hanging out with his English teacher so much.

"And besides," he continues, "I saw you kissing."

"What? When?"

He shrugs. "Lots of times. You didn't think I could see you, but I did."

I think back to the start of things, trying to figure out when Sam could have seen us, and I realize it was quite often.

At home, Nolan and I tried hard to keep things platonic with Sam around, but I don't think we were always intentional about it. It felt too natural being with him, and I didn't think to hide it because it never felt like it was something I shouldn't be doing.

"Oh." It's all I can think to say.

"Was it because I drank his PowerUp and borrowed his book?"

My heart squeezes for the second time tonight. "No, Sam, that's not what happened."

"Are you sure? Because Nolan was really mad at me. I thought he got tired of having me around and wanted us gone."

"We moved out because our apartment was ready early. That's all. As for Nolan and me…well, that's a little more complicated, but I promise it had nothing to do with you."

"Are you going to get back together? Because I really like him. He plays video games with me, and Dad never plays them at all. Plus, Nolan likes football, and Dad doesn't like that either. I liked having another guy around."

Hearing Sam's words…something hits me.

Nolan's been like a stand-in father for Sam. Losing him wasn't just a blow for me, but for Sam too.

"I could play video games with you," I offer, trying to keep the tears stinging my eyes at bay. "And I can learn about footsball."

"*Foot*ball," he corrects, then sighs. "See? This is why I need Nolan around."

I'd like him to be around too.

"What? Your mom not cool enough for you anymore?"

"Were you ever cool?"

"Hey, watch it! I brought you into this world, and I can take you right back out." I grin to myself. I always wanted to use that line.

He shrugs, unapologetic. "So, are you getting back together?"

Can you get back together with someone you were never really with?

Nolan and I were never supposed to last more than my stay. There's no getting back together.

There's moving on.

And that's what I need to do—move on.

I need to accept that Nolan doesn't feel the same way I do.

"No, buddy. We're not," I tell him, pulling into the school parking lot and pushing the car into park. "But let's not focus on that. Tonight is your night." I force a smile, turning to him. "You ready to go kick some ass?"

His lips are turned down in a frown, though I don't know if that's from my confession or because he's not looking forward to the performance.

"As I'll ever be." With a huff, he climbs out of the car.

We make the quick walk into the school. Sam goes backstage, and I head for the audience.

River and Dean are already there with seats saved. They wave frantically when they see me.

"Hey." I slip onto a chair. "Thanks for the seats."

"I made sure to get here early so we'd have a good spot," River says, beaming brightly, proud of herself.

"Excuse me," Dean cuts in, glowering at her. "I've been saving these seats since five PM…when I set the damn chairs up. You showed up five minutes ago."

"Like I said, I was early."

He glares. "You're lucky I'm a teacher and there are parents around so I have to remain professional—otherwise I'd flip you right off."

She pokes her tongue out at him and he reaches for it, trying to pinch it.

I swear, sometimes they're children.

"Yes, Dean, you're exuding professionalism right now."

My back snaps straight and my heart jumps into my throat.

Nolan came.

I glance up at him, and damn am I met with a sight.

Gone is his usual flannel. Tonight, it's replaced with a crisp, clean gray button-up with the sleeves rolled up, exposing those muscular forearms of his I know feel like heaven when wrapped around me. His long legs are clad in dark-wash jeans, and his usually messy hair is combed back. A dusting of facial scruff covers his face.

I swear he's more handsome than I remember.

"This seat taken?" He nods to the one next to me.

I shake my head, unable to speak.

He gives me a shy grin as he sits. When our shoulders brush, neither of us moves to give the other more room, both relishing the feeling too much to do so.

Dean leans forward, giving Nolan a pointed look. "Glad you could come."

Nolan's lips tighten with annoyance, but he doesn't let it linger too long. "Wouldn't miss it."

Tension lingers, thick and suffocating, and I miss the times when it was easier with Nolan, when nothing was strained between us and being with him felt as natural as breathing or loving The Beatles.

"Did we miss anything?" Caroline asks, sliding down the aisle of chairs, Cooper right behind her. She plops down in the chair next to Nolan. "We got held up. Someone came into the store five minutes before close."

"Good sale?" River asks.

Caroline nods. "Over two hundred."

River sits back with a smile, pleased.

"Where's Patrick?" Dean asks, checking the time on his phone. "It's about to start and Sam goes on fourth."

Frustration slams into me, and I try my hardest not to get upset all over again thinking about the phone call I received thirty minutes before we left the apartment.

Patrick couldn't make it...*again.*

He was bailing on his son...*again.*

"Last-minute work thing came up." I try to contain my anger when I say it, but the words still come out with grit.

Anger flashes in River's eyes and she opens her mouth to respond, but the lights dim and the crowd goes quiet. She settles back in her chair, shaking her head.

I understand her reaction. She's been there as much as I have to pick up the pieces when Patrick disappoints Sam.

"Told ya he's a fucking moron," Nolan mutters out of the side of his mouth, and my shoulders shake with laughter.

A sense of calm washes over me for the first time tonight. This feels normal with him. Feels good. Feels *right.*

The announcer hits the stage, and we focus our attention on the front of the room. The curtains pull back for the first act, and that's when I feel it.

Nolan's fingers ghosting down my arm.

He slips his hand under mine and laces our fingers together, pulling our joined hands into his lap.

My breathing stops, and I swear I feel his touch everywhere.

It's like coming home.

When I remember to breathe again, I peek over at him. He's staring straight ahead, attention on the stage in front of him. We sit like this through two more performances, him watching the stage and me watching him.

"Next up, we have Samuel Martin singing and playing guitar."

Everyone applauds politely…except for us.

"Yeah, big Sammy!" Cooper hollers, hands cupped around his mouth.

"Woohoo!"

"Go, Sammy!" Dean claps, whistling loudly and clearly playing favorites.

"Kick some a—"

I yank River back down into her chair, shaking my head at her.

"What?" She shrugs. "I was totally going to say butt."

"Uh-huh. Just sit down and quit embarrassing your nephew."

"It's my job to embarrass him," she insists.

I roll my eyes, turning back to the stage in time to see Sam take his spot. He places the guitar on his knee and adjusts his microphone stand.

Tears spring to my eyes, but this time they aren't sad ones. He looks so grown sitting up there, and I'm so proud to call him mine.

"Uh, hi," he whispers into the mic, and the audience giggles. He clears his throat. "This, uh, this is a song called 'Everlong' by Food Fighters."

"Did he just say *Food* Fighters?" River whispers, giggling.

He misses the first few chords.

"Shit," he mutters, and the mic picks up the feedback.

My cheeks flame as embarrassment floods me, but

everyone seems to get a good laugh out of it. Maybe I should have gotten onto him about the cussing after all.

He picks it back up, and this time he doesn't miss a single chord. When his voice carries through the makeshift auditorium, he has everyone's attention.

He's good, better than I've ever heard him before, and if I could bottle this moment in time to keep forever, I would.

Especially the part with Nolan being here.

When he squeezes my hand, I glance up at him. He's looking down at me, and I see it all in his eyes.

The regret.

The apologies.

Love.

For the first time since I walked out of his apartment, I have hope.

"I'm so proud of you!" I squeeze my son tightly, and despite being in public and having all his friends there, he hugs me back. "Second place is amazing! I don't know where you got those pipes. I can't sing for crap."

"Thanks, Mom. Dean's been teaching me some techniques on singing too."

"Guess that means we have to keep him around then, huh?"

"As if you had a choice." Dean holds his fist out to Sam. "Proud of you, bro."

"Thanks for everything, Dean."

He winks at him. "Any time. Just make sure you tell River

how awesome I am as often as possible. I could use the brownie points."

"You spoiled that one for yourself. Now I'll never believe a word he says about you," River says.

Dean's face falls. "Well, shit."

We all laugh.

"Mom, where's Nolan? Did he come?"

"He's…"

I glance around the room, trying to find him, but he's nowhere in sight.

Did he leave? How can someone as big as him disappear without anyone noticing?

My chest fills with disappointment.

"He came," River reassures him.

"And he wanted you to know he's super proud, but he had to get home. He has to be up early for work tomorrow," Caroline adds.

At least part of it isn't a lie.

He is proud of Sam.

I just don't know why he walked away…again.

I push away my dismay and slap on the biggest smile I can rally, hoping nobody notices how bogus it really is.

We all make plans to meet at The Gravy Train for a celebratory dinner, then head for our cars.

"Mom, what's that on the car?"

I squint, trying to make out what Sam's pointing to.

"No clue."

He runs ahead, excited and curious.

"It's a rose! And a note!" he yells. "But they got the wrong car. It's not your name on it."

With shaky fingers, I pluck the single rose from Sam and read the attached note.

Tonight, my sweet Juliet.

There's a flutter of excitement in my belly and an ache of longing in my heart.

Nolan.

I still want him.

"Why are you smiling? Should we find Juliet so she can get her rose?"

She already has it.

Chapter 20

NOLAN

It's just after 10 PM when I finally conjure up the courage to shut my truck off.

I stare up at Maya's new apartment building through the windshield. All the lights are off, and I have no doubt she's already snuggled in her bed.

I push open my door, and it creaks loudly in the otherwise quiet night.

On unsteady legs, I carry myself around the back of her complex, which backs up to a beautiful view of the same lake I once took a naked dive into in freezing temperatures just to prove a point.

That's why I'm here tonight too—to prove a point.

To prove to her I'm in love with her and I don't want to keep giving up on people before they can give up on me.

I walk down to the edge of the lake and pick up a handful of small rocks. Nothing too big or too sharp—I'm trying to be romantic, not stick her with a repair bill.

When I line my shot up with what I'm fairly certain is her balcony, I launch.

The rock skips off the glass door, and I wait a moment to see if she heard it.

Nothing happens.

I pull my arm back and send another rock soaring.

Wait.

Nothing.

Then another.

Wait.

Nothing.

My hopes dwindle as each rock lobbed bounces off the door with no response.

Maybe she's not home? Maybe they stopped off for a late celebratory dinner?

No. I know Maya, and there's no way she'd be out this late with Sam.

I toss another rock.

Wait.

Another.

At this point, all my ideas of grandeur are gone, but I can't seem to make myself give up yet. I'm tired of giving up. It's all I've ever fucking done.

I stretch my arm back one more time. If this doesn't work, it's time for plan B.

With a prayer, I launch the last rock in my hand.

It never makes contact with the door, because it's swung open.

"I called the police, young man!" An old lady who—clearly—isn't wearing a bra rushes out of her apartment, shaking a landline phone in the air. "They'll be here any minute! Don't you dare think about running!"

I want to point out that if she called the cops, she

shouldn't have told me so, because I'd definitely be running right now if I were a criminal.

But I'm no crook.

I'm just a man standing in front of an old lady, asking her which apartment his one true love lives in.

I take a step closer, cupping my hands around my mouth. "Do you know Maya West?"

"I said don't run!"

"I'm not running!"

"I'm warning you, mister!"

I hold my hands up. "I'm not fucking running!"

She gasps, her hand flying to her chest. "How dare you!"

I wince. Okay, poor choice of words.

"Sorry!" I shout. "I'm sorry! I'm just looking for—"

A light flicks on next door and the patio door is pulled open.

And my whole world snaps back together.

Maya steps onto the balcony, light illuminating her, making her look like the angel she is.

"Nolan?" She crosses her arms over her chest at the cold, bitter air. "What are you doing out here?"

Did she not get my note? "Did you not get my note?"

"I did. I figured you'd use the door though…"

"Who is that over there?"

Maya turns to her neighbor. "Hi, Ms. June. It's me, your new neighbor, Maya."

"The one with the little shithead kid always playing that damn guitar too loudly?"

Maya chuckles. "That'd be the one."

The old woman grumbles something I don't catch, then pushes her shoulders back, tipping her chin up. "Well, what are you doing hanging around with some riffraff like this? Throwing stones at people's windows—he could have broken one!"

"I'm sorry, Ms. June."

She points a finger. "You should be! I was sleeping and having a lovely dream about Denzel Washington before your little friend went and ruined it." She crosses her arms over her chest, huffing. "I'm going back to bed."

She storms into her apartment and slams the door, no doubt waking others up.

"Did she say she called the cops?" Maya asks me. I nod, and she sighs. "She always threatens that, but she never actually does."

Thank fuck. I'd rather not have to deal with that right now.

"Why are you throwing rocks at my neighbor's window, Nolan?"

"I was trying the whole Romeo and Juliet thing. You know, getting all romantic on the balcony and whatnot."

"Should I be reciting Shakespeare? Because I don't think I know any."

"Nah. Could never understand anything he was saying anyway." I glance to her neighbor's patio, where I see the old bat peeking through her blinds, phone up to her ear. "Fuck. I'm pretty sure your neighbor is calling the cops on me for real this time. Knew I should have gone with the boombox bit."

She chuckles. "What song would you have played?"

"To get you to come out here? All of them. I'd have stood out here all night to get you to listen to me."

"It's freezing."

"It is. But trust me, life without you is a lot colder than this."

I see her throat bob, and she rubs at her arms. "What do you want, Nolan?"

My nerves come back full force, and fucking hell is it embarrassing how hard I'm breathing right now.

She stands there, arms crossed, brows raised, waiting patiently on me.

"I...I..."

I lift my hand, rubbing the back of my neck. My hands are literally trembling. My chest is shaking with fear.

But there's no turning back now.

"I'm an idiot."

She huffs out a laugh. "Tell me something I don't know."

I smash my lips together, tucking my hands into my pockets. "Okay. I deserved that one." I tip my head back to meet her eyes. "When my mom left and I had to watch my father live without her all those years, it fucked me up. I didn't want to become him. I didn't want to hand myself over to anyone as fully as he did. I couldn't stand the thought of being so...broken. So, other than Dean because that asshole wouldn't leave me alone no matter how hard I tried, I pushed everyone away. Always. I did it for so long that it was second nature."

She watches me with rapt attention, hanging on to every word.

"Then you happened, and I realized what a complete fool I was."

Her lips part in surprise, gray eyes shining with curiosity.

"I was a goner the first moment I laid eyes on you, and I think deep down, I knew it even then. You were like this magnetic force pulling me in from the start. I *had* to know you. Even if we'd met that night how we were supposed to, it would have been the same way. There was no way I was going to walk out of the bar that night not knowing you. It almost felt like fate when you needed a place to stay and I had the room."

I wet my lips, shaking my head.

"I swore to myself I would keep my hands to myself, said nothing would happen between us because I knew I couldn't give you what you wanted. But we both know how that turned out, huh?"

She dips her head, and I don't have to be standing next to her to know she's blushing, thinking of all the nights we definitely didn't follow that rule of mine.

"And that's just it, you know? It took nothing at all to break my resolve because being with you was the easiest thing I've ever done. It was like I was built to exist next to you, and all those years I spent pushing everyone away was because I knew somewhere out there, you were waiting."

I can see her breaths in the cold air, her chest rising and falling with anticipation.

I exhale slowly, rocking back on my heels. "I guess what I'm trying to say is, I'm sorry for pushing you away. I'm sorry for running. I'm sorry for being an idiot, and I'm sorry I didn't do this sooner. But I'm not sorry for falling crazy in love with you."

She doesn't say anything.

Doesn't move.

"Did, uh, did you hear me?"

She nods, then spins on her heel.

The door slams against the frame and the panic slams into me all over again.

I'm shaking, and it's not from the cold. All I can do is stand there and stare up at the empty balcony.

What the fuck just happened?

Of all the ways I thought this could go—and I had *a lot* of scenarios run through my head—this wasn't one of them.

I'm frozen to the spot. Can't seem to get my legs to move.

I should run after her, right? Go to her. Make her see that I'm serious. That I want her. That I'm not going anywhere.

I hear hushed footfalls crunching against the frosty grass, and I swivel toward the sound.

Maya's standing a few feet away wearing those old, ripped-up leggings again and a t-shirt. No jacket. And no shoes either.

I cross over to her, ready to sweep her into my arms and take her back into the warmth of her apartment. "What are you doing? It's freezing out here. You're—"

"Did you mean it?"

"Yes. I—"

She crushes her lips to mine, her fingers crashing through my hair, and I drag her to me, circling my arms around her, vowing to never let her go again.

She pulls away first. "Say it again," she demands, lips still ghosting against mine.

"I love you." She sighs blissfully, pressing our foreheads together. "And not just you. God help me, but I love that shithead kid of yours too." She giggles. "I've missed you both so much these last few weeks."

"We missed you too. It's been so miserable without you. I think Sam mopes as much as I do."

"I'm sorry," I tell her again. "I'm so fucking sorry, Maya. I should have never let you leave. I should have never made you feel like you had to leave."

"It's okay."

"It's not." I pull back, looking into her gray eyes. "It's not okay. I don't want to love you the wrong way. I want to do it the right way because you deserve that and so much more."

Our bodies fit together like that's what they were made for, and our mouths tangle in a heated kiss.

It's not until she's trembling under my touch that I remember she's not dressed for this weather at all.

I pull away, needing to get her warm. "We need to get you inside."

She nods. "One more thing?"

"Yeah?"

"I love you too…" I grin against her lips. "*Romeo*."

244

Epilogue

MAYA

I'm sixteen all over again, sitting on the toilet in my best friend's bathroom with pregnancy tests scattered all around me, waiting to see if my world is going to be flipped upside down again.

"Oh god."

"What does it say?" River strains to see over my shoulder. "What does it say?!"

"It's negative."

She sinks back against the counter, looking as relieved as I feel. I exhale a breath, all the stress that's been weighing on me for the past three days dissipating.

I take two more tests for good measure, and they all give the same result: *negative*.

I realized earlier this week my period was late. It took me two more days to get up the courage to say something to River and another day to muster enough to take a test.

"Same?" River asks.

I nod. "All the same."

"Oh, thank god." She straightens. "I mean, this *is* a good thing, right?"

"It's definitely a good thing."

It's only been six months. Nolan and I haven't been dating near long enough for me to be pregnant with his child. Hell, we're not even living together yet.

Not to mention I'm not sure how Nolan feels about having kids with me. I know he's not a big fan of them, but he loves Sam so much. Maybe his feelings have changed?

"You know you have to tell Nolan about this, right?" River chews on her lip, apprehensive.

I sigh, not looking forward to it one bit. "I know. I'll tell him tonight."

I pull my phone out of my purse, which is sitting on the bathroom counter.

Me: Still on for dinner tonight?

There. Simple enough.

No reason to get him freaked out while I'm still freaking out.

Romeo: Pizza?

Romeo: I'll bring the meats.

Me: *rolls eyes*

Me: But deal.

Romeo: Be home in a bit.

Smiling, I tuck my phone back into my purse and push up from my spot on the closed toilet lid.

I wrap my arms around River. She stumbles, not expecting the affection, but squeezes me tightly anyway.

I'm not sure how long we stand there hugging, but it's just what I need.

"Thank you." The words aren't much, but they're important ones, and she knows how much I mean them.

"Always." She gives me another squeeze before releasing me and wiping at her eyes. "Fuck. That shit got me emotional. I was having flashbacks to being sixteen."

"You too, huh?" I laugh, brushing away my own tears. "At least this time I would have been a little more prepared for it."

"You'd definitely need a bigger apartment."

"And car," I add, stepping in front of the mirror.

I'm a mess. My hair is all over the place from me running my hands through it, and my makeup is a wreck from rubbing at my eyes so many times.

Despite my appearance, I feel a million times better than I did when I first entered the bathroom.

I love Nolan, but I'm not ready for a baby. I want it to be just us—and obviously Sam—for a while.

"River! I'm home!" Dean's voice echoes through the apartment. "Where are you?" He moves closer to the bathroom, his voice growing louder. "So, listen, I was thinking we could try that thing you mentioned the other night in the bedroom. You know the one I'm talking about. It's dirty as hell, but the more I think about it, the more turned on I am."

I lift my brow at River, whose face is burning a bright red.

"Shut up," she hisses to me, and I laugh. She yanks open the bathroom door, running smack-dab into Dean. She slaps her hand over his mouth. "Stop talking!"

His brows crease together, confused. Then he slides his eyes my way, and they widen to twice their size.

Slowly, River removes her hand.

Dean swallows thickly, shoving his hands into the pockets of his khakis, nodding at me. "Maya."

I smirk at his discomfort. It's not often Dean is knocked down a peg or two, so I'm going to enjoy the moment while I can. "Dean."

"What, uh, what are you doing here?"

"You know, just…stuff." I shrug. "What's the dirty bedroom thing?"

"You know, just…stuff," he mutters.

I laugh. "Well, this has been a mildly enlightening experience, but I'm going to get upstairs. Nolan should be home before too long."

Dean steps out of the way, and River leads me to the door.

"I expect a full report later," I tell her.

"Likewise."

I give River another hug, thanking her again, and head for the elevators. I step inside when one arrives and press the button for Nolan's floor, settling in for the slow ride.

This slow-ass elevator is about the only thing I don't miss about this building. The rest? I miss it so much. Especially waking up next to Nolan every morning.

At the time, living separately sounded like a good idea. We wanted to take things slow. Wanted to ease into everything.

But now? I miss him like crazy.

We still have dinner together every night—either at my place or his—but it's getting harder to walk away from him each night.

I want more with him. But I'm scared he's not ready yet.

The elevator finally reaches his floor, and I make my way

down the hall to Nolan's door, passing by the apartment that's been raising a lot of brows lately.

Dean's younger sister, Holland, moved into the building two weeks ago, and whoever she's rooming with…well, let's just say they are *not* friends. I don't even live here and I've heard the gossiping and complaining about them always fighting.

I slip my key into the lock and push inside.

"Hey!"

"FUCK!" I scream, clutching my chest and falling back against the door.

"We can, but after dinner. I'm starving."

"What the hell, Nolan?!" My chest heaves as I gulp in air. "You scared the shit out of me!"

He shrugs. "Told you I'd be home in a bit."

I push off the door with a sigh. "I didn't expect you to be home *that* soon."

"Surprise?"

I glare at him and he laughs, crossing the apartment to me. He doesn't stop until I'm pressed up against the door. On instinct, my hands curl around his neck, and my legs go around his waist when he slides his hands over my ass.

I giggle as he buries his face in my neck, kissing and nipping at me until he reaches my lips. He takes my mouth in a heated kiss until I'm writhing against him, dying for a release.

Then he relents, making his way back down to that spot I love.

"Well, hello to you, too," I say.

He pulls back, grinning at me. "I missed you."

"Yeah?"

He nods. "Just a little bit."

I swivel my hips, feeling his very obvious erection brushing against me. "It doesn't feel like a little bit."

He lifts his brows. "So you want to play that game, huh?" He drives into me, and my eyes roll back in my head. "I win."

I shake my head. "You don't play fair."

"You love it."

"I love *you*."

He sighs. "Say that again."

I grin. Over the last few months, Nolan hasn't shied away from showing me his affection at all. Sometimes I swear he enjoys hearing the words *I love you* more than I do.

"I love you," I whisper, brushing my lips across his.

He smiles against me. "I love you too. You hungry?"

I swivel my hips again. "Starving."

He laughs, setting me back down on the floor. "I meant for pizza."

"But I thought you were bringing the meat?"

"Always, but dinner first. There's actually something I want to talk to you about."

Just like that, I'm reminded I have to tell him about the pregnancy scare.

I won't lie—I'm a bit nervous. We've been doing so well together these last six months, and I don't want to do anything to rock that boat.

He chuckles and uses his thumb to pluck my bottom lip from between my teeth. I hadn't even realized I was biting it. "Stop looking so worried. It's a good talk…I hope."

"Yes, because tacking on *I hope* makes it so much better."

He smacks my ass. "Come on. Let's go eat."

I toe off my shoes and follow him into the kitchen.

He puts two slices of pizza on my plate and loads his own up with four, then grabs a bottle of ranch from the fridge because he's not a savage.

We sit side by side at the bar top and tuck into our meal.

I'm about done with my first slice when I can't take the silence anymore.

"I need to talk to you too."

He freezes, a slice of pizza halfway to his mouth. "Are you breaking up with me?"

"What?" I shriek. "No! No way!"

He wipes his forehead with the back of his hand. "Phew."

"But...I, uh, took some pregnancy tests today."

"Oh god."

He pales, and I laugh.

"They were negative."

He visibly relaxes. "Thank fuck." He drops his pizza to his plate, turning to me. He spins me toward him, reaching for my hands. "I mean, if you were, I swear I'd be happy with that too."

Tears spring to my eyes at his words. "You would?"

His brows crush together. "Of course I would. I love you, Maya."

"I know you do, but I also know you don't want children."

"I have a child."

Warmth spreads through me.

Sam.

Nolan's love for my son knows no bounds, and it makes me so fucking happy. There is never a moment I doubt how he feels.

When Nolan and I started dating, he sat down with Patrick to have a conversation about what his role in Sam's life would be. He didn't want to step on his toes but wanted to be there for Sam as a second father figure.

I swear, I fell even more in love with him at that moment.

"But this would be different."

He nods. "It would be. And, okay, at first I probably wouldn't be too excited about the idea. But I'd love the baby no matter what and would take care of him or her. And you."

"I know you would. I wouldn't marry you though."

He tips his head in an unasked question.

I shrug. "The first man who asked me to marry him did it out of obligation. Look how that turned out."

He slips a hand up my cheek, fingers sliding into my hair. "When I marry you—and yes I said *when*—it won't be because I feel obligated. It will be because I love you more than I could have ever imagined, and I'll be damn sure to remind you of that every day."

My eyes well with tears again, and he sweeps away the lone drop that falls down my cheek.

"Got it?" he asks.

I nod. "Got it."

"Good." He drops his hand. "Now, are *you* okay? With the tests being negative?"

"I am. I mean, a part of me loves the idea of having a baby with you someday, but I want that someday to be off in the future. You know, after we have basic things figured out like our living situation, so we aren't going back and forth between apartments all the time."

"Speaking of that…" He clears his throat. "That's kind of what I wanted to talk about."

My heart flutters in my chest.

Is he…

"As you just said, we're always traveling back and forth, and it kind of sucks. I know we said we wanted to do slow, but this shit is starting to kill me. I want to go to bed with you every night and wake up to you every morning." He licks his lips and flicks his eyes away. "And so…"

He trails off again, and I can tell he's nervous.

"Are you asking me to move in with you?"

"Yes…but I'm also asking you to buy a house with me."

My mouth falls open. "A…h-house?" He nods. "Like a real house?"

Another nod. "Yes. I drove past one the other day and—"

"The white brick one with the gray door and giant porch? On Gardener?"

"How'd you know that?"

"Because I saw it the other day too. As soon as I got home, I took a virtual tour and spent at least two hours planning our life in it."

A slow smile spreads across his face. "I got yelled at today because I was on my phone looking at it."

"Seriously?"

"Yep. And then on my lunch break, I called the realtor, and she said there are no offers yet."

"Little presumptuous, huh? How do you know I'd say yes?"

He lifts his shoulders. "Because you love me."

I do. So much.

I never thought I'd find someone who makes me as happy as Nolan does. Even when I don't like him, I love him. And that's all I ever really wanted out of a relationship—someone who respects me, loves me, loves my kid, and wants to grow together instead of apart.

He reaches for me, pulling me off my stool and into his lap with ease. I slip my arms around his neck as his fingers play against my lower back.

"So, what do you say? Want to buy a house together?"

So badly. But the reality is, Nolan makes a lot more money than me. I'm not sure I'm financially ready for something like a house.

"I don't have a ton of savings," I tell him.

"I've been saving for a place for years. I can take care of the down payment."

"I'm not sure how I feel about that…"

"Do you trust me?" he asks, and I nod. "Then trust me that we'll figure it out. I don't ever want you to think it's not your place too. We'll make all decisions together and we'll split things as evenly as we can. If at any point you don't feel comfortable, you say the word and we'll stop and re-evaluate."

My heart swells. "How did I get so lucky with you?"

"I am pretty amazing, huh?"

I laugh, and he swallows the sound with a kiss.

He doesn't pull away until we're both out of breath.

"So?"

"Keep kissing me like that and I'll buy a hundred houses with you."

"I said I have a decent savings, not that I'm a billionaire."

"Well, then this definitely won't work out."

I try to push away from him, and he locks his arms tighter around me.

"Nice try. You can't get away that easily."

"Not for lack of trying," I pout.

He rolls his eyes. "So, you did a virtual tour, huh?"

"Oh yeah. I practically have the place memorized."

"Did you happen to see the…"

I grin, knowing exactly what he's getting at. "Balcony?" I nod, dropping my head against his. "I knew I had you pegged right, Romeo."

His lips brush against mine as he whispers, "Only if you'll be my Juliet."

Thank you for reading **CRAVE THY NEIGHBOR!**
Next up is Tempt Thy Neighbor, an enemies in the workplace/roommates romcom!
Order TEMPT THY NEIGHBOR now so you don't miss it!

Missed Dean & River's story? Keep swiping for a preview of **Loathe Thy Neighbor**…

Other Titles by Teagan Hunter

ROOMMATE ROMPS SERIES

Loathe Thy Neighbor

Love Thy Neighbor

Crave Thy Neighbor

Tempt Thy Neighbor

SLICE SERIES

A Pizza My Heart

I Knead You Tonight

Doughn't Let Me Go

A Slice of Love

Cheesy on the Eyes

TEXTING SERIES

Let's Get Textual

I Wanna Text You Up

Can't Text This

Text Me Baby One More Time

INTERCONNECTED STANDALONES

We Are the Stars

If You Say So

HERE'S TO SERIES

Here's to Tomorrow

Here's to Yesterday

Here's to Forever: A Novella

Here's to Now

Want to be part of a fun reader group, gain access to exclusive content and giveaways, and get to know me more?

Join Teagan's Tidbits on Facebook!

Acknowledgments

My Marine. I love you. This past year has been challenging in so many ways. I'm only glad that even after spending more time together than we ever have in our entire relationship, we haven't killed each other. (No, really, FBI. It wasn't me.)

Laurie. Thank you for being my brain. I'd be nowhere without you.

Caitlin. I can't shout from the rooftops loudly enough to explain how much I adore you. Thank you, thank you, thank you.

Julia and Judy for those extra eyes on this baby. I can't imagine publishing a book without either of you now.

Kristann. Thank you for always being there no matter what time of day or night it is. My life wouldn't be the same without you in it.

Bloggers & Bookstagrammers. Your support means so much more than I can say. Thank you for sharing every cover, release, and announcement. You're the real MVPs here.

Tidbits. Thank you for always being there to make me laugh and keep me going.

Reader. I love you. I know there are many authors and books out there, so thank you for taking the time to read this one by me. Giving me a few hours of your time means so much more than you could know.

With love and unwavering gratitude,
Teagan

TEAGAN HUNTER is a Missouri-raised gal, but currently lives in South Carolina with her Marine veteran husband, where she spends her days begging him for a cat. She survives off of coffee, pizza, and sarcasm. When not writing, you can find her binge-watching *Supernatural* or *One Tree Hill*. She enjoys cold weather, buys more paperbacks than she'll ever read, and never says no to brownies.

www.teaganhunterwrites.com

Printed in Great Britain
by Amazon

61033765R00158